Cover Design Created By:

Samantha Thomas
&
Audrey Adasiak

HUGO READ THIS!

/// *Brandon Swarrow*

iUniverse, Inc.
New York   Bloomington

Hugo Read This!

This is a work of fiction. All of the characters, names, incidents, organizations, and dialogue in this novel are either the products of the author's imagination or are used fictitiously.

iUniverse books may be ordered through booksellers or by contacting:

iUniverse
1663 Liberty Drive
Bloomington, IN 47403
www.iuniverse.com
1-800-Authors (1-800-288-4677)

Because of the dynamic nature of the Internet, any Web addresses or links contained in this book may have changed since publication and may no longer be valid. The views expressed in this work are solely those of the author and do not necessarily reflect the views of the publisher, and the publisher hereby disclaims any responsibility for them.

ISBN: 978-1-4401-4272-7 (pbk)
ISBN: 978-1-4401-4274-1 (cloth)
ISBN: 978-1-4401-4273-4 (ebook)

Printed in the United States of America

iUniverse rev. date:5/6/09

CHAPTER 1

When number six ran out onto the football field on that humid Monday night in San Diego, every person in the crowd stood up and screamed. Some fans rubbed their eyes in disbelief. They have eagerly anticipated this moment for a very long time. The passionate fans were shocked and excited as they pumped their fists into the air for the first time all evening. After a first half filled with mistakes, the crafty veteran quarterback put a towel on the back of his neck and took a seat near end of the bench with his team facing a 31 – 7 deficit. The impatient crowd would have been ecstatic to see any change at the quarterback position at this point. But this wasn't just any ordinary signal caller entering the game.

His name was Hugo Brody and he was born and raised in the sunshine state. He was groomed to be a great quarterback by his father, former NFL quarterback, Sebastian Brody. Hugo shattered many records throughout his high school and college careers, and the San Diego Chargers rewarded his efforts by making him the first player selected in this past year's professional football draft. He signed the largest contract ever given to an NFL player despite never competing in a single game, thus further enhancing his celebrity status. Hugo Brody's name was a common topic of discussion throughout our proud country. Men and women in California, as well as the rest of the United States, talked mostly about his natural skills and ability, his cannon arm, his raw talent, and when the Chargers will hand him the reigns. However, he was also making a name for himself off the field with his flashy persona, male model looks, and luxurious lifestyle.

He wore the number six to remind all of his fans of the prediction he made live on national television just seconds after being selected number one at the professional football draft. Hugo quietly walked up to the microphone stand after he was selected, held up a Charger jersey and said, "I will bring the city of San Diego six Super Bowl rings while I'm here." The replay of his incredibly bold comments aired continuously on sports channels for several weeks. Some sports analysts laughed at his notion and publicly called him out, while other reporters and advanced scouts said that he was one of the most talented players they've ever seen come out of college, and that they wouldn't bet against him.

The media circus that followed Hugo Brody, and all of the hype that had been built up since the beginning of the season, had made the moment when he took the field even more extravagant. Even though the score was 31 - 7 at halftime, and Hugo was basically coming into the game for "mop up duty," it was the first real action the Chargers young star quarterback had seen. He hadn't taken a single snap and this was already San Diego's seventh game of the season.

He trotted out to greet his teammates in the huddle like a proud trophy whitetail buck who knew his antlers were the most spectacular. His long dark hair poured out from the back of his helmet and waved to and fro as he jogged. The linemen welcomed Hugo into the huddle and the semicircle closed around him. One of the announcers broadcasting live on national television said, "You could just feel the electricity in the stadium." The young, confident quarterback flapped his arms in a downward motion as he broke from the huddle to silence the roaring crowd. Hugo placed his hands under center to receive the snap and calmly scanned the left and right sides of his line. His voice echoed powerfully, "Twenty-one, twenty-one, hut, go!" The center snapped the ball with fury and within seconds, Hugo Brody fired a bullet ten yards to his tall, speedy wide receiver. He completed his first professional football pass and from that point on Hugo never viewed another game from the sidelines.

He orchestrated one of the National Football League's most memorable comebacks that night in his inaugural game. He looked masterful completing pass after pass. Confidence and determination dripped from his chin strap in the form of perspiration. His wide receivers continuously glanced at their hands after making catches to see that they now resembled swollen plums. The team celebrated the incredible win by hoisting the young quarterback onto their shoulders, but even as they enjoyed that invigorating moment, the team was already anticipating moving forward with this unearthly talent.

Hugo smiled and celebrated with his teammates. However, as he sat upon their broad shoulders, it seemed almost as if he had foreseen the very moment. He did not seem over zealous. Hugo just sat above his teammates relishing the victory with a deliberate grin on his face. The crowd continued at a constant roar even until well after the game was over. Hugo Brody began his professional football career just the way he knew he would; victorious. The television broadcast crew pronounced the game "The Monday Night Miracle," and from that day on the Chargers knew that they had found their guy.

CHAPTER 2

Hugo and the Chargers played exceptionally well for the remainder of the season and made the playoffs for the first time in quite a long time. Hugo never cooled off. He was unstoppable, breaking rookie records set by some of the all-time greats. He quickly became the face of the franchise, and in many ways the face of the National Football League. Although the Chargers did not make it to the Super Bowl in the young quarterback's first season, the team won its final ten games and gained valuable playoff experience that they could hopefully build upon. Football fans across the country eagerly anticipated Hugo's first full season as the starting quarterback. They saw what he was capable of in the small ten game sample season and were salivating for more Hugo Brody.

The 23-year-old athlete won his first ten consecutive games in his second season as a starter and made good on the first Super

Bowl promise. In an extremely close title game, Hugo threw his fourth touchdown pass in overtime to win the championship in dramatic fashion. He was voted the Most Valuable Player of the Super Bowl, and in that same season the phenom went on to receive various honors such as league MVP. He was even awarded a trip to Hawaii to represent the AFC as their starting QB on the All Pro team. He was sitting on top of the world with his feet dangling just out of the reach of the other professional quarterbacks of his time. To the Hispanic population in San Diego he quickly became known as "Hugo El Milagro," which translates into Hugo "The Miracle" Brody.

Expectations for Hugo's second full season as a starter could not be any higher. Anyone who follows the game of football was interested in his every move. Six Super Bowl titles didn't look all that unrealistic anymore. His performance on the field continued to exceed everyone's expectations. His performance off the field was becoming more and more legendary by the day.

His celebrity status exploded, and ascended higher than some of the most elite movie stars. His handsome face was exploited heavily by advertisement agencies, and was highly sought for endorsements. He was a young, fearless, sophisticate who was mysteriously new to the entertainment scene. Women began to form a rabble hoping to catch a glimpse of their future husband hours before and after his games. He received hundreds of letters and emails per day, most of them containing phone numbers or wedding proposals. Beautiful women would even go as far as to send him sensual portraits and explicit pictures. He couldn't go anywhere without being recognized, and if he did try to get into a club or restaurant, scantily dressed women and paparazzi suffocated him. Despite the numerous distractions, Hugo Brody kept piling up the victories on the field for the Chargers.

He led San Diego to their second consecutive Super Bowl Championship and once again was named Super Bowl MVP. The improbable was happening right in front of the eyes of the sports fans. Hugo's immaculate story was blossoming into herculean fairy tale. He had taken the league and the world by storm. Hugo has had just two full years in the league as a starter, and already had compiled two unbelievable Super Bowl Championships. Once again the young superstar took his seat upon the throne that his teammates created with their shoulders. However, being so famous began to take its toll.

The off-field frenzy was getting so out of control that the superstar decided to preemptively hire a bodyguard. He was able to locate a mammoth of a man that was just known to the public as SWAT. SWAT was a mysteriously enormous specimen who made Hugo's linemen on the Chargers look like horseracing jockeys. He stood close to seven feet tall and weighed about 450 pounds. He was quiet most of the time, but when he did speak, his voice was ferociously deafening. Hugo was never spotted in public without SWAT firmly attached to his hip. Much of the general population had never seen or heard of SWAT, they just continually made assumptions based on his name and demeanor. One reporter for *People Magazine* wrote that the giant bodyguard was given his nickname by the public based on what he does to reporters and photographers who create obstacles in his associate's path. He simply just "swats" them away like miniature merciless mosquitoes.   Another columnist of an established San Diego newspaper suggested that SWAT received his name based on his years of service as captain in the SWAT Special Forces unit. Nobody has ever confirmed or denied such reports; however, it is undoubtedly clear that Mr. Brody had become so immensely popular that even his enigmatic protector became a prominent fixture in the daily headlines.

CHAPTER 3

Hugo grew increasingly more comfortable with his new bodyguard. He seemed less tense when it was time to deal with the media. The constant hounding was one result of stardom that Hugo had difficulty adjusting to. He did not want to devote his precious time continually answering questions or posing for pictures, and SWAT made an immediate impact when it came to controlling the press. SWAT also believed that as a bodyguard he must also focus a great deal of attention to two certain types of fans. He categorized the two groups simply as either "jealous" or "obsessed." Since the quarterback began receiving hate mail and threats on a daily basis, SWAT thought that it would be in his client's best interest to monitor these particular situations closely. The bulk of the hate mail was mostly from men who were jealous, or upset, that their team was just thrashed by Hugo and the boys. The obsessive variety was almost always from female fans who'd had sports enthusiasts for husbands. In a sick and demented way, the giant bodyguard found amusement in reading the piles of obsessive mail that continuously poured in from the ladies. SWAT recorded the total number and frequency of each repeat sender and often times became absorbed in his sifting.

Although many of the fiendishly obsessive messages were unique in their own way, some were extremely strange and bizarre. These fanciful messages were SWAT's favorite and sometimes the big guy would even laugh out loud while reading them. His laugh began to stir quietly in the depths of his stomach and then erupted so loudly that it was sort of awkward to hear the large fellow. He would share, "Yo' Bro' listen to what dis' chick says she'd do for ya." Then directly after reading the message, he would burst into his deep, sinister howl. Hugo even flashed a roguish smile once in a while when reading what some of the girls would *do for him* or *do to him*.

One particular female fan tried exceptionally hard to get noticed. She caught the attention of both men with her infinite number of email and text messages, as well as her ability to track his every move. The men also couldn't help but to notice the overall amount of effort and diligence she had put into her personalized messages. She even had the audacity to call his cell phone once in a while. How she managed to get his phone number perplexed the two men regularly for his number was ever-changing. Hugo never did listen to what she had to say. He would simply hang up the phone as soon as she introduced herself, and then promptly proceeded to change his phone number. Even though he reportedly had been seen with a multitude of various beautiful women, rarely did he ever spend enough time with any particular one of them. Rather, he deprives his dates of any knowledge that may go beyond the physical realm, or the surface layer. It baffled the quarterback how this one particular girl had known auricular little secrets about Hugo Brody that very few people could have known, and that's what made her such an anomaly. SWAT showed concern; and often times referred to her as the most dangerous type, yet remained astonished by her persistence.

She went by the name Monica Resser, and Hugo affirmed to his giant buddy that he had never met her. SWAT facetiously suggested that it may be possible he had forgotten her name due to the sheer volume of women who have passed in and out of the superstar's life. Hugo did not deny the fact that he had always been quite the gigolo, but also said the chances are highly unlikely that the two had ever crossed paths. The young quarterback did give quite a bit of thought to the name Monica Resser, only because SWAT made such a huge deal of it. The truth was; he did not remember any girls named Monica. Going back year by year, Hugo revisited faces of girls whom he had had relations, but failed to match a face to Monica. Together, the star and bodyguard concluded that this most obsessed fan (MOF) probably goes by an alias. The only way they would ever truly know who Monica Resser was, would be to meet her in person. Neither Hugo nor SWAT had a desire to meet this loser, psycho-stalker.

During the off season they devoted an evening to examining some of the clues left by the MOF. All of Monica's email messages and letters were very well written grammatically with an advanced and at times elevated vocabulary. The correct grammar separated itself as a clue mostly because ninety-nine percent of the other messages were dreadfully mistake laden. Obviously this MOF was an intelligent woman. Another clue was the actual content. She never sounded way too incredibly obsessed in her messages like other fans. She never did say that she loved him, wanted him to be the father of her child, or would do *anything* to be with him. She mostly just wanted to meet Hugo in person. She attempted numerous times to set up meeting places such as upscale restaurants, or clubs. The last curiosity that was deemed a clue was the fact that Monica had said numerous times she was hurt, or upset by the fact that Hugo did not remember her. Her approach was clever.

CHAPTER 4

Hugo resembles his father in more ways than one, especially when it comes to the ladies. Both were blessed with refined princely appearances as well as magnificent charm, fine taste, and a celestial presence that only encompasses the most natural superstars. They shared the uncanny gift to be able to communicate profoundly as if everything they said were the climax to a wonderful story, and it was effective in winning over any type of audience. Both father and son usually left the listener wanting more, whether it was desired initially or not. They also had in common the same love em' and leave em' type of attitude. Sebastian Brody was married three times and tried capaciously to instill in his son's brain that most of the women he will meet are concerned only with money. He advised Hugo to be very cautious in choosing his close relationships.

Sebastian gained full custody of Hugo when he and his third

wife were divorced. Hugo doesn't remember his birth mother, nor has he ever even seen a picture of her. He was only two years old at the time, and Sebastian's explanation for the separation was always simple. He said that his mom became a money worshiper, and a "powda nose" or in other words, drug addict. Hugo has asked him questions several times about his mother and Sebastian always replied in a similar manner, "Don't worry about it; your mother was a zombie."

Sebastian Brody had always been a very honorable and righteous man. If there was one thing he couldn't bare witness to, it would be another human being throwing the gift of life away by using or abusing drugs. He was bewildered by the stupidity of addiction, and he just flat out loathed those weak individuals who allowed themselves to become fiends. Sebastian admittedly loved Hugo's mother very much and always believed that he could've dealt with a materialistic money addict, but he just could not envision himself trying to handle a junkie dissipating their existence on a daily basis.

He began to worry about his son's off the field lifestyle. He heard rumors of wild parties at his residence, and would even brazenly question Hugo about the parties while meeting for lunch or dinner. Sebastian had repeatedly told Hugo throughout his life about the dangers of drugs. He had even been known to get aggressive on occasions claiming that he would "break his neck if he ever saw his eyes glowing like the parallel zeros on his alarm clock."

Hugo and his father had a very strong relationship. Hugo had the utmost respect for his moralistic father, and admired him enough to decorate an entire wall in his office with his father's photographs and his past football memorabilia. They had always shared a unique father-son, mentor-mentee bond. However, when Sebastian said that the parties must come to an end, the budding star obeyed his father's commands only for a short time. He also shrugged off and shielded himself from the guidance provided by his own teammates and coaches. He was young, single and enjoying life to the fullest. Hugo saw no harm in having a little fun once in a while and for the first time in his life; he began to lie to his father. He ignored Sebastian's reverberated warnings and he started to openly deny the soirees that he had been having.

Despite Hugo's erratic behavior off-the-field, he still carried the Chargers on his wings to an incredible third consecutive Super Bowl title. It was a very difficult game against the Seattle Seahawks, and Hugo was swept out of the stadium by SWAT so he didn't have to deal with all of the press. Hugo was exasperated and needed some time to relax and recuperate. He left everything on the field this season and just wanted to get home to his no stress zone. He was now halfway to achieving that one time ridiculous goal of winning six Super Bowls. He was like a man amongst boys on the football field. He showed no signs of slowing down. His strong arm, pinpoint accuracy, and knowledge of the game put fear in the eyes of defensive opponents.

After several days of idleness, Hugo hosted a party in honor of his third Super Bowl victory that was nothing short of legendary. It lasted for nearly three days and may have continued even longer if super sleuth, Sebastian Brody hadn't surprisingly burst in.

Sebastian's unexpected and unannounced visit prompted a series of enormous changes in the life of Hugo Brody. Sebastian insinuated through the propped open front door with extreme caution. He couldn't hear anything except intermittent bursts of laughter above the hip-hop music blaring from the speakers. Then he saw it. He froze as if an elephant was charging toward him. There was some *THING* dancing in the living room on one foot in tight circles that resembled his son. He was nude, wearing nothing but a pair of gigantic sunglasses. The crowd that had assembled to witness the father-son confrontation began to uproariously erupt into laughter. Hugo didn't even notice his beloved father standing in the doorway. He just kept spinning, but now on both feet because he was losing his balance.

Others took notice of Sebastian Brody's awe-stricken face, and their laughter ceased as they suddenly left the room thinking that there may be a slight chance he would detonate. However, to everyone's surprise, he didn't react at all. He just stared at what used to be his baby boy, shocked by his sinful behavior. Sebastian didn't move a muscle for nearly five minutes and did not even blink. The bass from the stereo rattled his teeth. His dark grey and charcoal color hair turned a lighter hue. Hugo still never noticed his father (or he pretended not to see him). Sebastian turned to exit and for the first time since his own childhood the skin on his forehead started to tighten and tears began to stream down his cheeks. The honorable Sebastian Brody, a man known by many as somewhat of a renowned orator, left without saying anything.

A few days passed and the brooding Sebastian debated

internally about how to resolve the situation. He wanted to forget the whole thing, and just call to check on his son. He decided that if he were to ignore the incident, the insane behavior may just continue. He did not want to see his only son throw away everything and become part of the zombie squad. He was determined to help his son return to the self-possessed man he once was.

It was strange for the two of them to go a full week without talking, so Sebastian felt compelled to call him. Sebastian did not discuss the incident over the phone at all, and politely requested his son's presence at lunch later that day. Hugo willfully agreed to meet his father for a bite to eat and to converse.

They met at a small local restaurant chosen by Sebastian, ironically dubbed Pardon's Pub. As Hugo hastily rushed toward his reserved seat across from his father who was coincidentally rested at table six, he abruptly began apologizing to the man he has so much respect for as he sat down. His slumping posture and his outward emotion were signs of remorse for hosting the parties. He said that he thinks someone might have slipped some type of poison into his drink. He swore that he had not knowingly taken any type of drug, and declared that he never would.

Sebastian was convinced that this was all an act as he digested only portions of his son's pathetic apology in disgust. He focused directly on Hugo's lack of eye contact and could tell that this ignorant man sitting across the table from him was not his son anymore. Sebastian was by no means a detective, but he knew his own son inside and out. This impersonator walked differently, talked differently, and most of all, barely resembled his divine son. When the honest Sebastian Brody could sense the transformation taking place, his muscles all contracted simultaneously as he gasped loudly and covered his mouth with his unused napkin. His worst nightmare was coming true and it startled him. He became cognizant of the fact that his entire life's dedication may be slipping from his fingertips and it deflated him like a punctured helium balloon. A sinister metamorphosis in both men had emerged from this luncheon.

Chapter 5

Despite Sebastian's cautionary counseling, Hugo's quest for bliss off the field continued, and on occasion intensified. Sebastian heard countless rumors that were endlessly being spread throughout the community about his only son. Repeatedly, Sebastian requested his son's presence at a particular lunch date or dinner in an attempt to quell his reckless behavior. Hugo remained obedient, and attended each and every session. However, in these convocations, unfortunately more and more distrust began to develop between father and son. Hugo admitted to his commendable father that he was indeed having these massive parties at his home, but he also continued to openly deny any type of drug use. He said, "Dad, there may be some people there doing it, but I'm not one of them. I do like to have a few drinks at social gatherings, but that's it. I swear!"

Sebastian placed his clenched fist; thumb first, over his tight lips with repugnancy. It prevented him from saying something that he might later regret. He pondered over what his response would be as he lowered his temporary hand clutch from his mouth. He calmly picked up is beverage from the table, took a small sip, and in an utmost authoritative voice said, "Hugo, I have worked very hard to preserve our good name in this community. You simply are not doing your best to protect it at this particular juncture. Surely, I do not need to remind you that you are under a national microscope as well. Just welcoming those types of people into your home serves as proof that you can be influenced or persuaded. Now, what can I do to help you son?"

Hugo abruptly replied, "There is nothing to resolve father. There is no existing problem. I dedicate myself to football. I continue to train rigorously every day, I am still on an athletic diet, and I see nothing wrong with having a party or an occasional drink. Honestly, I'd like for you to stop breathing down my neck and let me live my life a little." Hugo snapped out of his momentary rant as if he couldn't even believe he just said that to his father and he continued with, "my friends and I thought we had a prowler, or a stalker on our lawn a few times this month already Dad, but SWAT told me it was just you. You need to relax. I understand your concern, and I appreciate it, but everything will be O.K., trust me." Hugo scampered out of the restaurant clearly agitated, leaving his father just sitting in his chair shaking his head in disbelief. Sebastian remained convinced that his son was taking part in something immoral, and the fact that he could blatantly lie to the man who raised him, fueled his abhorrence.

Several months later, and well into his fourth football season,

Hugo met with his father again. This time the get-together was requested by Hugo. When he arrived, he was not as well-groomed as the general public was most accustomed. His dark beard had disbanded all over his face, and his long, straight hair once full of body, was now matted down resembling greasy feathers. Sebastian was once again found snooping around on the premises on a number of occasions, and Hugo wanted to voice his displeasure directly to his father about his constant meddling. His first words as he passed through the entrance of the small town restaurant reeked of desperation, "I no longer want my father sneaking around my house trying to catch me doing something wrong. If it was anybody else but YOU lurking in the shadows, my bodyguard would have had you arrested by now. It's embarrassing father." Sebastian attempted to chime in, but Hugo would not permit his verbal lashing to cease. His voice grew louder and even more emphatic, and he began to draw the attention of other patrons. He said, "Dad, you have been examining my behavior from a distance and it is really becoming creepy. Your intrusiveness bothers me and the fact that you don't trust me anymore because I like to have parties at my own house is just wrong. You are an unreasonable man." Hugo truly believed that he was not doing anything to warrant concern. He managed to calm himself when he looked into his father's eyes and saw penance for his prolonged prying. This was the first true eye contact that the two kinsmen have shared since the conversation had started, and it was brief.

The visual connection halted the moment Sebastian sucked in his upper lip with the aid of his bottom teeth and allowed his head to fall. Sebastian had goose bumps at this point because he realized that this was a battle he could not win. He continued to peer toward the floor as he said sadly, "Son, I shall stop trying to intervene. I am sorry. You are an adult now, and can make all your decisions on your own. I'd like for you to remember this one little piece of advice though; rendering yourself to sin and betrayal shall instantaneously light the fuse of horrific karma. Keep your nose clean boy, or I'll be the least of your worries."

Before leaving the establishment, the sensational quarterback broke the news to his unforgiving father about his plan to relocate. He informed him that he had purchased a newer home in a secluded area in northern California approximately two-hundred miles away from the town in which he was raised. He also added that a few modifications had to be made to the existing property, and that he won't be able to move for at least a month, but already had begun packing.

Again Sebastian was left speechless and stunned. He thought about questioning his son's commitment to their relationship. He considered asking his son if he was indeed the reason for the sudden move. But oddly enough, he mostly just reminisced. He viewed image after image in a daydream state as if he was watching a highlight film of the fondest memories that a father and son could have experienced with one another. The news broke the old man's heart, and he couldn't help but to feel partially responsible.

Hugo glanced one more time at his father as he left. He noticed changes to his father's physical appearance as well. His posture slouched similar to a giant salamander attempting to sit upright; his chin nearly touched his tie as his eyes struggled to follow his son's exit. He looked older, and he was exhaling slow but loud. Hugo's heart filled with remorse as he waved goodbye to the stern old man. A sudden deep compassion swarmed over him like he was almost forced to say something. He felt compelled as if he owed it to the poor guy to cheer him up. So in a lamenting tone, Hugo said, "Don't worry Dad. I'll invite you up to visit when the place is finished and I'm all moved in."

CHAPTER 6

(THE DONJON)

It was an incredibly hectic and stressful month for "El Milagro." He packed hurriedly for two weeks straight after compiling his fourth consecutive Super Bowl Championship. He didn't even have time to celebrate this particular Super Bowl win over the rival Seattle Seahawks, after all, the victories became essentially expected. Also, before the playoffs started, Hugo signed a lavish contract extension that would keep him in a Charger's uniform for the next five years, as well as pay for his luxurious new mansion. He had been pestered endlessly by the media and the general public for almost five years now, and he truly anticipated moving into such a private residence. Of course SWAT would move in with Hugo as well. He became much more invaluable to Hugo as time went on, and SWAT really went out of his way to prove to his employer that he was trustworthy. SWAT routinely saved him time and money. He was the individual who organized a few of his close burly friends to actually plan and carryout the big move. He didn't seem too keen about having a careless moving company come in and recklessly bounce all of Hugo's exquisite belongings. SWAT's friends were tedious and careful with each and every object in an effort to try to preserve its value. The only payment that they were interested in receiving was an autographed Hugo football for each of them and pizza with extra mushrooms on it.

Even though the star quarterback and his massive body guard kept a business-like relationship on the surface, the pair had developed quite a strong bond of friendship over time. SWAT's opinion was valued, and Hugo allowed him to be actively engaged in the decision making process. In fact, many of the alterations that had to be made to the property were adopted by SWAT for heightened security reasons. He also wanted to design his living arrangements to be acceptable for his taste, and suitable for a man of his stature.

They named the house "The Donjon" because of its half-castle, half-fortress appearance. The massive structure nested at the top of a hill and was previously owned by a Hollywood actor and actress that split. It was only six years old and hardly looked lived in. The establishment came with ten acres, which SWAT had fenced in with a ten foot tall iron barrier. It also housed a newly renovated fitness center complete with an indoor basketball court, spa and swimming pool. Hugo particularly treasured the kitchen area. Its vastness alone was one of the main reasons why he desired and pursued the property so intently. He believed that if his whole offensive line wanted to spend some time at his place, he'd better have enough space to accommodate all of the titans while they gorged. The colossal kitchen was basically the size of an average middle class family's house. It contained two side by side stainless steel refrigerators; a breakfast area that seats twelve, hand-carved oak cabinets, marble floors, and a custom built stainless steel double basin sink that one could wash a large pet in.

SWAT was given the freedom to install the most sophisticated security system that technology could produce at the time. The system included a silent alarm, twenty-four cameras, and two rover C-Robs. The C-Robs were exclusively designed by the military and the abbreviated term stands for "conscienceless robots." The C-Robs were released only if the silent alarm was sounded, or if there was a breach at the main gate. The robots were armed with an overhead spotlight and camera that targeted and recorded any movement with infrared sensors. The C-Robs were also programmed to neutralize the perpetrator with a tranquillizer gun that is capable of shooting up to one hundred feet. Hugo and SWAT argued about the excessiveness of the robot rovers, but SWAT had convinced his boss over time that they would ensure his safety. Hugo would sometimes make jokes to his gigantic friend about the robots. For example, if they had leftovers, Hugo would sarcastically say, "If we had dogs instead of these stupid robots, we could feed *them* all of these delicious table scraps."

After living in The Donjon for a few weeks, Hugo decided that it was time for his father to come up to visit and tour his new residence. He called Sebastian and gave him the address. He told his father to come up as soon as he is able to. He also mentioned that he missed him already, which probably accelerated his father's decision to drop everything at once and drive north. He told Hugo that he missed him very much too, and that he may need to do a little apologizing upon his arrival. Sebastian sounded extremely excited over the phone, and told his son that he would be there tomorrow evening.

The gravel driveway to The Donjon was about a quarter of a mile long, and anybody inside of the house can detect even a slight disturbance in the serenity from a significant distance. Even more so at night, where one could clearly hear the resonance of smaller stones squeezing between tire tread, and spot the headlights of a vehicle entering the drive from far beyond the trees. Hugo was eager to see his dad. They were both able to forgive and forget their differences and even to some degree learn and grow from it. He was spirited to see the headlights of his father's truck enter the drive. He gazed at the camera posted atop the main gate from inside the house to catch a glimpse of Sebastian's face. Once he was certain it was his father, he climbed out on to the front porch and greeted him with a firm handshake and a slight one armed embrace. They sat only for a few minutes and discussed the drive, but Hugo was anxious to take his father on a tour to show him what he was so proud of. They visited each room, with Hugo acting as a guide showcasing all of the recent changes that have been made. He also pointed out where his father could sleep for the night, but purposely left the basement and the C-Robs off the tour to avoid any questions of lunacy. Sebastian's eyes were completely open in amazement; even though he admitted several times that he was tired. He was overwhelmed by the sheer size of the house, as well as the superior attention to detail. Hugo said after the tour concluded that he could not take all of the credit, his bodyguard SWAT had helped with just about everything.

Just then, SWAT turned from his desk and shouted jokingly across the room, "It was all me Mr. Brody! You know "El Milagro" over there doesn't care what his place looks like on the inside." SWAT then followed his comment with the typical dark, uneasy laughter. The big guy often found it hilarious to use the title that the Latin population had bestowed upon his employer.

Hugo and his father had a brief discussion about the mansion, and Sebastian decided that he would go up to his bedroom for the night. Hugo followed him up the spiraling stairs with his bags. Hugo felt like he wanted to say something to him about their last few meetings, but before he could make a remark, Sebastian said, "Goodnight son, I'll see you in the morning."

At the crack of dawn, Sebastian already had the entire residence reeking of bacon. He slowly cooked breakfast and the two men sat down to talk. Sebastian mostly discussed the fourth Super Bowl victory, and his son's gorgeous new home. They never brought up anything that had occurred in the past that morning. Forgive and forget. Each man knew that they had made some mistakes, and those mistakes were communicated nonverbally throughout the whole visit. "The house symbolizes a fresh start for you son, and I'm proud of you," said Sebastian. "But, I do have one piece of the past that I brought with me on this visit. Come outside with me, I wanna show you what I found." Both father and son paced out of the house to Sebastian

Brody's truck. Sebastian said excitedly, "Do you remember what you used to take aim at when you were a kid?" Hugo just looked at his dad strangely. Sebastian reached into the bed of his truck and pulled out the tattered old mannequin that his son used to throw footballs at for hours at a time when he was a young child. It looked exactly like Hugo remembered it, yet much more weathered now that the mannequin's flesh had turned a weird brownish-yellow hue. Even though Hugo truly did not want this creepy old dummy, he felt like he couldn't break his father's heart once again. He noticed that his dad even took the time to put a fresh new Charger's jersey on it, number six of course, so without a moment's hesitation, he accepted it.

Hugo pseudo-smiled and said, "Thanks Dad, I'm going to put it right over there in the yard."

Sebastian told Hugo, "Thank you for being so hospitable. Your house is incredible, and I am very proud of you son." He gave his son a firm goodbye handshake, boosted himself high into his truck, and waved one last time as he was granted permission to exit through the heavy automatic gate.

As Sebastian's truck became smaller and less audible, Hugo took a moment to study the mannequin's disturbing features. He did not recall the dummy having two large shadowy eyes when he was younger. "They look like two dark mirrors now," he thought to himself. He attempted to recollect any positive memories associated with the mannequin, but failed. Instead, he remembered being a vulnerable young child and his father basically forcing him to throw nearly five hundred footballs at the dummy wide receiver.

He would take aim and fire ball after ball as Sebastian Brody shouted, "Hit him in the chest! I said, in the chest boy!" He remembered those few instances where his arm felt like it was going to remove itself at the shoulder, and when he told his father about his sore appendage, he was ordered to run the monster hill in the backyard. Also, directly linked to this hideous mannequin were strong recollections of times when Hugo would get upset or angry about something, slam the front door, and heave orbs of hate toward its chest.

Truthfully, he detested that old mannequin. However, he did make the promise to his father that he would indeed post the epitome of dreadful memories somewhere in the yard. He decided to place it across the field, about as far away from the house as possible, and just barely visible from the front porch.

CHAPTER 7

After the slightly cordial visit from his father, the big shot quarterback felt a renewed sense of alleviation. He was free-spirited and completely unrestricted. He spent weeks creating a carefree atmosphere, surrounding himself with companions who shared the same euphoric goal. The frequency of his parties during the off-season went from taking place occasionally on weekends, to almost every night, with each night's gathering taking over as party of the year. Some of the regular attendees never even left Hugo's house, and practically began to live at the open Donjon for weeks at a clip. Hugo began drinking much more heavily. He was no longer in peak physical condition, and needless to say his workout regiment was lackluster at best. Most of the time, he would sleep during the day and repose in preparation for the next evening's fiesta. He was living in a fantasy world where money was endless, a dependence on alcohol did no harm, he could choose any attractive sexual partner he desired, and had little or no responsibilities.

The most adorable females flocked to Hugo's house nightly for his exclusive parties. Celebrity men and the world's most prominent sports figures would appear dressed in their most expensive suits. Each man entered the door with a beaming smile. As they entered, they permeated the air behind them with their own secret trial of predatory cologne. Popular singers, bands, and some of the most talented DJ's would provide free entertainment just for being afforded the pleasure to attend. The seclusion of The Donjon gave people in the public's eye the perfect place to go and mingle. They viewed each night as an opportunity to fuse with other luminaries in similar industries. More importantly, Hugo's galas dually served as a place where the prominent masses could go to for a secretive release. The atmosphere was almost always vivacious and convivial. The blend of wealth and taste of those in attendance was evident in each person's hand, where exquisite cocktails, wines and posh martinis were most commonly spotted. This aristocratic crowd continually played an important factor in the mood. Just as the saying goes, "the more money, the more problems."

In the early stages of The Donjon's existence, the games and activities were very much harmless. Of course, wagering of any kind was a favorite form of entertainment among the affluent. Spectators would bet excessively on televised sporting events, shooting baskets in the indoor basketball court, and even high stakes casino-type games. For the most part, the monetary adventures remained fun and lighthearted with all intentions favoring the morality of the participants involved. However, it did not take very long for the elite to become too satiated with the typical festivities and soon the contests grew more intense. In a very short amount of time, these non detrimental jollifications became uninteresting, which in turn led to far more bizarre revelries. Some would argue that the events being staged at Hugo's Donjon at this point were borderline perverse. For example, two rumors swirled in relation to the games being played at Hugo's Paradise. One story claimed that a football competition between striking, young sprites took place regularly on an intentionally superfluous muddy field behind the mighty Donjon. What made these games even more spectator friendly was the fact that the female participants wore only helmets, shoulder pads and shoes. The weekly entertainment television station first broke the story, and the ordinarily bubbly blonde on television's weekly entertainment insider even appeared visibly repulsed as she read the story aloud from the teleprompter. Gossip positively circulated as well for the blessed MVP of these games. For this beauty's dreams would be fulfilled later on in the evening underneath Hugo's satin sheets.

A second, more disturbing tale had also leaked to the public. It involved an unusual requirement in which each female contestant must hold a paper thin-walled sixty watt light bulb in her mouth while performing various acrobatic challenges. No common citizen could possibly understand why any type of event like this would take place, nor could the everyday person wrap their head around why any pretentious young female would exploit them self in such an improper way. However, the commoners of the community were even more bewildered when they heard that it was their beloved Hugo, himself, who had created the sport to identify which beauty had the softest mouth. Newspapers and magazine companies, who have long been looking for any inside material on these renowned gatherings, or any more dirt on America's favorite quarterback, began fanatically printing stories without sources. Half of the general public was appalled at Hugo Brody, yet the big shot's most devoted fans stood by his side and were disgusted by the articles that were rapidly being printed. Hugo's faithful fan base remained steadfast constantly dismissing the propaganda as "all lies." It is amazing to see in today's society how many people continue to adore those particular individuals who are undeniably cocky and overtly boastful. The millions of people who admired and supported Hugo Brody should shoulder some of the blame for fueling his arrogance.

One notable weekly magazine printed a detailed article specifically about the light bulb challenge based on an anonymous witness account. The spectator claimed that while observing one of these absurd competitions, one young girl leaped the highest over the high jump bar out of all of the other contestants, but her teeth made contact with the bulb upon impact of landing, and it violently exploded in her mouth. Despite leaving the party to seek medical attention, and most likely stitches inside of her mouth, she did not even win the grand prize. The ultimate prize, Hugo, eventually went to the babe who orally protected her bulb from shattering throughout all of the events. The anonymous spectator and author of the article seemed to be more in disbelief that the injured girl wasn't at least awarded some kind of consolation prize, rather than focusing on the fact that these repulsive and indecent games were occurring. Entertainment television was guilty as well, focusing primarily on the actual contests and games, rather than the fact that these events were utterly demoralizing for those involved. It was known that most of the participants in these grotesque events were not celebrities of any kind, so it wasn't such a big deal. The majority of competitors were young female fans who were not only promised party entry, but actually had an opportunity to accompany their idol to bed if victorious. Despite the scandalous press, and the possible damage to Hugo's reputation, the parties, games, and outlandish contests continued.

SWAT was assigned the daunting task of regulating who would, and who would not be granted access to attend the feral blowouts. He would question and comb the assembly standing outside the main gate each night to find the handful of lucky girls who were to be approved for entry. Sometimes, SWAT would make the girls dance for him, and then he would formulate selection based on which female impressed him the most with their skills. It was certainly a sight to see the contortions of envy upon the faces of the other self-proclaimed glamour girls when their name or number was not chosen. These were the types of girls who had been accustomed to having their needs satisfied practically all of the time, and the instant when they were denied admittance, they would display fits of anger that one would normally associate with a foot-stomping, back-arching toddler. SWAT quickly grew tired of this tedious obligation, so he approached his boss about hiring some additional bodyguards that he knew very well and considered trustworthy. Hugo, assiduously appearing in commercials now, agreed that they should employ more assistance; therefore he did not deny his large friend's request. SWAT added two new members to the establishment, who were also his closest friends. The men turned out to be the same bulky beefcakes who Hugo met once before when they aided him in his great move. Hugo remembered their faces, immediately saying, "Large pizza, extra mushrooms," upon greeting his new employees. The combination of the sudden hiring of the two brutes, Big Cane and Marinky, as well as allowing them to live permanently in The Donjon, would not only save on time and efficiency, but negatively it stands as Hugo's first crucial, yet dreadfully careless, mistake. Big Cane and Marinky became responsible for smaller security issues such as enforcing the "no recording policy" while special events took place. Marinky was a very mild temperamental person who was laid back most of the time, and didn't say much. However, an incident during one of the soft mouth challenges occurred where a visitor to The Donjon pulled out his cell phone and deviously tried to record a video of the ladies. Marinky whistled to Big Cane who then raced through the crowd, grabbed the man's phone with his left hand and delivered a blow to the guy's chest with his right arm all in one motion. The sneaky camera man was stunned as he stumbled backward. Before he could even attempt to orally justify his actions, Big Cane swiftly smashed the phone off of his corpulent kneecap into about a dozen pieces. SWAT and Hugo complemented both men for their actions, as well as their enforcement of the rules. All four men worked well together, and developed a strong camaraderie. It was SWAT's crew, but they would all remain loyal and obedient to their superior, Mr. Hugo Brody.

CHAPTER 8

(THE REBIRTH, ALMOST)

With Hugo's fifth full season of professional football starting in just a few days, the haughty quarterback was in the worst physical condition of his life. His drinking had become almost uncontrollable, he was smoking cigarettes, and his diet consisted of mostly pizzas with cheese and extra mushrooms. He was still very much content with his lifestyle, but a few strange occurrences had begun to weigh heavy on his conscience.

Hugo was often seen with an alcoholic beverage in his hand, and was known to be quite hilarious when tipsy. However, over a period of three or four nightly gatherings, he made an effort just to sip, or social drink. But, as each night progressed, he became more and more inebriated. He couldn't recall the number of drinks he had consumed, but he was certain it was only a handful. He grew concerned because he was completely aware that this could very well be one of the signs of an alcoholic.

He knew that libertines cannot just have a drink or two, because once consumption begins, they do not cease until utterly intoxicated. He was worried that he may have a problem, but did not remember drinking a large quantity. He was cognizant of the fact that maybe his body was not digesting the alcohol in his system appropriately, and possibly his health could be at risk. Overall, Hugo was just bewildered by how he could get so wasted off of just a few drinks.

Another unnatural occurrence had also taken place over the last few nights. Hugo made it a habit to frequently step outside onto his porch to get away from the crowds, and have a cigarette. He has heard a crow calling out at all hours of the night. It is true that a crow will revisit the same place where it has lost its young and call for it repeatedly throughout the night. It is unavoidably distracting to Hugo's ears even more so because it defeats the purpose of fulfilling the need for peace and quiet. Even though he became so annoyed by the crow's call, and he was becoming more and more confused about his own tolerance, he did treat these bizarre happenings as individual signs to slow down a bit and concentrate on his brilliant career.

Hugo Brody gave the orders to SWAT and the crew to tone it down a little at The Donjon during the season. The men seemed a little upset by the requisition, yet reluctantly complied. SWAT decided that he will make an announcement to all visitors that tonight's bash will be the last big party until further notice. And that all events would resume at the conclusion of the upcoming football season. They did not want to deal with a major upheaval from their discontent friends. So SWAT, Marinky, and Big Cane met and discussed the best possible modus operandi to relay Hugo's message and came up with a three point plan. First, give them the news early, so the party can be treated properly as a grand finale. Secondly, all three bodyguards will make their presence felt while delivering the news. And lastly, reiterate the fact this is not the end of great times, just a postponement. The crew's plan was solid and at 8:00 p.m. they stepped up onto the DJ's equipment, ceased the music, and used the DJ's microphone to address the large and boisterous crowd. The heads of the masses turned in a synchronizing sweeping fashion as the music cutoff. SWAT cleared his throat and brought forth the news. The taut bodyguards cracked their knuckles and necks in preparation to suppress any vehement behavior, but none ensued. There were some angry countenances among the mob, and some devastated deportments, but for the most part the message was received without a hitch.

The grand finale went very well. No issues evolved and Hugo stayed sober all night. He was even the winner of the game called the "The Terrific Thong Toss" where participants would sling women's underwear twenty-five feet up to the ceiling while trying hook the thong onto a pointed edge of the overhead chandelier. The bodyguards remained on edge and conspired together all night long possibly discussing strategic plans or different scenarios for if a problem should arise. Their behavior was seen as odd on this particular night considering that the burly bodyguards are usually the first to take part in any type of foolishness.

As the season progressed, Hugo played exceptionally well even though he was tempted and eventually lured into sinful behavior on more than just one occasion. Considered a major turning point in his life, "El Milagro" realized in this his fifth season, that he was capable of playing great football and performing at a high level even with a careless party lifestyle. He was being compared to Babe Ruth for his ability to match his historical accomplishments on the field, with a reputation of an undisciplined and reckless American icon off the field. Even though his level of play was not as flawless as it has been in the past, once again Hugo led the Chargers to an insurmountable Super Bowl victory over their hated rivals the Seattle Seahawks. He really started to believe that he was untouchable at this point. He proved his arrogance time and time again. From publicly admitting to winning his fifth championship on "no sleep for a week," to purchasing different color Lamborghinis for himself as well as SWAT, Big Cane and Marinky. He had his notorious touchdown celebration patented so no one else could duplicate his histrionic pillory pose. He now embraced the spotlight. He welcomed all public interviews and forums usually with outlandish and obtrusive caveats such as bringing two or three women on TV with him. He would now allow photographs to be taken at any time wearing obscene clothing considered too edgy even for a rock and roll star. He went from a reserved role in a few commercials, to endorsing fallacious products such as cigars, cigarettes and even cheap liquors. Hugo Brody was no longer cautious. He scoffed at boundaries and consequences, and he certainly no longer cared about his image.

CHAPTER 9

As expected, after the season was over, the wild parties resumed at The Donjon. Only now Hugo was so out of control that he made yet another critical mistake. The boss gave the orders to his bodyguards to deny NO ONE's admittance. The Donjon was being trashed, the parties were preposterous, and Hugo and his crew were just completely smitten with what was taking place. They were devoted to debauchery and embraced all forms. There were no limits. The local police, the ATF, the FBI they were fully aware of what was happening at that mansion, and as soon as they were given some justification, they would spring into action. They were beginning to build a solid case when Sebastian phoned his insensible son and requested that the two meet for lunch at about the halfway mark near Twentynine Palms. It was one last desperation intervention on the part of Sebastian Brody, and he was pleasantly gratified to hear his son consummate his request. It was a surreal yet solitary drive north for Sebastian. He recounted, reenacted and rehearsed everything that he was going to tell Hugo. The importance of the meeting was slightly blanketed by the temporary schism between the two men, and Sebastian thought that he could use that to his advantage. He knew that if he could restore communication based on some small talk, then soon after capturing his son's attention, he would deliver the lecture of his life.

Hugo's ride south couldn't be any more opposite. Similar to a college road trip with young men en route to a spring break resort, Hugo and the crew took their party to the road. The four men were carelessly flinging empty containers at signs, singing along obnoxiously to every song playing on the radio, hollering obscenities at anything feminine, and laughing like school children. However, the joyful antics soon gave way to an unusual and unnatural event. After drinking almost an entire case of beer, the mirthful men were forced to pull to the side of the road to relieve their brimming bladders. On both sides of the roadway, where the vehicle came to a halt, there were steep canyons. The three beefy bodyguards all urinated close to the vehicle while Hugo staggered over near the cliff's edge. He was just inches away from the threshold swaying side to side and urinating.

As Hugo teetered, SWAT rushed to finish and yelled over to his boss, "Hugo, don't you fall off that ledge. It looks like its all rock down there."

Hugo responded with, "Maybe it's about time I become one with the ground." This statement prompted SWAT's immediate action and he ran over and stood right next to his unsteady comrade.

SWAT said dubiously, "Come on man, you still have way too much to do in life. Now, let's go." Hugo slowly began to turn around, but then stopped. He had this bemused look on his face as he now stood with his back to the enormous ravine. He carefully inched closer to the edge. The heels of his wobbly sneakers were making contact with no ground.   A tiny bit of gravel loosened and fell down the steep side just beneath his feet.

Hugo looked at SWAT and muttered, "Seriously, why do people always jump face first? Why not jump so you could land on your back? You could pretend that there are arms or pillows or something down there waiting to catch you." Then Hugo Brody seemed very sober as he said, "And, you could watch everything get smaller."

SWAT was clearly getting agitated as he interjected, "What are you talkin' about? Get away from the edge, man and quit actin' so stupid."

Hugo said, "Why don't you run down there and catch me? Come on, you are my bodyguard right?

SWAT replied, "Ya' I'm your bodyguard, but you're acting LIKE AN IDIOT! Now, let's leave!" SWAT knew at this point that his acquaintance was out of his head, so the giant slowly started to creep within an arm's length.

Hugo rambled on, "If your job is really to protect me then you'd better get down there. I can't balance myself much longer." SWAT then violently grabbed Hugo's shirt near where it covered his chest, and proceeded to drag him by his shirt toward the car. Hugo thrashed and flailed as he repeated, "I just think it would be cool to watch everything and everybody get smaller. I wasn't *really* gonna jump." With Big Cane's assistance, the huge bodyguards tossed the frustrated quarterback into the back seat. The only other comment made about the incident occurred shortly afterward as the automobile started cruising down the highway once again.

Marinky said, "Now we're gonna be late for the date." After about ten minutes of silence, Big Cane found a familiar song on the radio. The men started singing once again, and the wild and raucous behavior seemed to have gained momentum. The odd event that had occurred on the cliff was never mentioned again.

SWAT openly denied several of the men's requests for another rest stop, and they made it to Twentynine Palms. Hugo said that his father would be at The Wonder Garden. The second SWAT put the oversized vehicle in park, all four guys jumped out and raced into the restaurant. As the men rushed for the restroom, Hugo noticed his solemn father sitting at a small table for two. Hugo bolted past his father and shouted, "I'll be right out!" Sebastian was left sitting there surprised and perplexed. He caught a strong wave of booze as the men stampeded by. He knew SWAT, but was totally unfamiliar with the other two ogres. All four men came out of the bathroom at the same time. SWAT pulled another small table next to the one Sebastian rested his elbows on, and the others dragged chairs in from nearby empty tables. Sebastian, visibly upset, knew that he was short on time so he skipped the small talk and launched into his lecture. He didn't really want the other men to hear what he was about to tell his only son, but he thought that his message might inevitably benefit the whole group of misfits. "You are taking the life out of me son," Sebastian said. "Your sinful behavior is killing me. Every drink you consume is one less breath I take. I did not raise you to be like this. I quit blaming myself." Sebastian paused to check his son's face for any possible reaction. He saw none and then his rant continued. "Look at yourself, you're a mess. You are killing yourself as well. The parties, the drugs, the booze; it has to stop. Go to rehab or something. Please, do it for me (your father), your fans, and for most of all, YOURSELF! You must make better decisions. Now, what do you have to say for yourself son?"

Hugo, seemingly disinterested, took his time to respond as he pretended to canvass the menu. Eventually he did reply. He said, "I'm happy, and that is what you need to accept. I am in a perfect place right now, father. I appreciate your concern. I really do, but this is how I want to live my life." Just then Hugo got up from his chair and said, "Are you guys ready? Nothing looks too good on the menu here."

A very angry Sebastian Brody stood up as well and said in an increased volume, "Where are you going? I am not finished discussing this with you!" Hugo and his crew just kept strolling toward the exit. Sebastian blurted one last significant shred of advice as his son turned and walked away. He exclaimed, "I'd like to say that I will see you again one day my fine son, but separate paths have been chosen."

The Wonder Garden was nearly empty, but an ominous

silence descended upon the patrons and workers. The only sound resonating from the establishment was the bell ringing on the entrance/exit door four times. Those four vexations sounded eerily similar to the final bells heard at the end of a championship heavyweight fight.

Without introducing his new friends, without ordering any food or drink, just like that, Hugo was gone. He had driven several hours only to converse with his own caring father for about one lousy minute. And according to his dear old dad, Hugo seemed to be defunct in more ways than one.

Sebastian thought seriously about getting in his car and following the four fools. Soon after Hugo and his crew vacated the parking lot, Sebastian did indeed follow them but only for a short time. The men stopped at another restaurant called the Palm Inn. The tender father once again faced the complicated dilemma of whether or not he should intervene. He sat in his car and pondered over what could he say or what he could do that would possibly change his son's awful conduct. He felt absolutely helpless as he peered through blurry tears from a distance toward the main entrance to the Palm Inn. He knew that if he tried to snatch his son and try to drag him to the nearest rehabilitation clinic, the bodyguards would just toss him to the side. His sorrowful heart was barely beating, yet his trembling hand managed to push the gear shift into drive. The decision to leave his son, and all of his vile indulgence, was probably the single most difficult and painful choice he had ever been called upon to make in his entire life. As he passed the Palm Inn, the old man's lips moved but only a faint, final farewell whisper could be detected. He feebly murmured, "Good bye my sacred son."

Chapter 10

(The Mysterious Note)

Hugo Brody and his band of bodyguards wasted little time after disregarding the fatherly advice. They checked into the Palm Inn and rapidly resumed their excessive partying at the pool bar. The small tiki area around the pool was near filled to capacity, and many of the occupants recognized Hugo and SWAT. The population soon began to annoy the men with a barrage of autographs and a desire snap photos so they were forced to order a few drinks and go up to their rooms a little earlier than they would have preferred. One particular female even followed Hugo and the crew into the elevator. Collectively the men were irritated by her presence; however she adamantly denied any type of pursuit and stepped off the elevator on the sixth floor. As the four men rode all the way up to the top floor presidential suite, they commented on the beauty of the young girl. SWAT even jokingly remarked, "El Milagro, I can't believe you didn't invite

her up. She looked kind of cute in that short little denim skirt."
Hugo, using the wall to hold him up, was clearly too inebriated
to jest back. Marinky and Big Cane actually had to help the
disoriented superstar walk from the elevator to the room. They
crashed there overnight.

The next morning the men traveled quietly north and returned
to the extravagant mansion that the four of them call home. As
their vehicle slowly crawled up the long narrow drive, SWAT
noticed something unusual about the mounted security keypad
and camera. Taped to the keypad was a letter apparently intended
for Hugo eyes. It was a fascinating note with each individual
letter cut out of a magazine. It captured all of the men's focus as
SWAT removed it. He passed the note to his employer, punched
in the security code and passed through the massive iron gate.
SWAT parked, and despite a long ride, no one stepped out of
the vehicle. They were each taking turns examining the curious
letter that read:

After concentrating on the foreign document for a short while, the befuddled men concluded that they recognize some of the names, and that it was a compilation of dead celebrities. Big Cane also discovered that the largest characters running vertically spelled out his manager's full name. Hugo carried the strange note with him into The Donjon and placed it on the island in the center of kitchen. He said, "Leave this letter right here. I want to do a little research on these names. Oh, and SWAT, see if you can retrieve any footage from one of our surveillance cameras. I'd like to know who was brave enough to put this note on my house."

CHAPTER 11

Hugo and his imposing chief guardian retreated to the security station where monitors and digital recorders can be viewed. SWAT immediately began to rewind the footage. Both men were eager to find out who the perpetrator was. They paid particularly close attention to monitors one and two anxiously awaiting anything unusual. The footage had only been rewinding for a short time when Hugo exclaimed, "Stop it, I saw something!" SWAT pushed the stop button and, according to the timer at the bottom, it read 5:55 in the morning. The two men didn't even want to blink as the moment that they had been anticipating grew near. 5:56 am nothing. 5:57, 5:58, nothing. But as soon as the clock at the bottom of the monitor changed over from 5:59 to 6:00 a.m. Hugo and SWAT witnessed something almost unexplainable. At six o'clock in the morning, camera one, which was observing from high atop the main gate, captured an older black hearse blazing up the driveway leaving a cloud of dust swirling about. The hearse came to a screeching halt just a few feet away from the security keypad and camera. A frail old man got out of the car before it stopped rocking back and forth from the action of shifting it into park. Both SWAT and Hugo's eyes were arid as they watched in amazement, and to some degree disbelief. The small security room was like a sauna from the heat rising up from the all of the digital equipment. A tall, thin older man wearing an all black suit with matching jacket emerged from the settling dust. The pressed suit looked to be the darkest shade of black as it contrasted against the mysterious old man's pale skin and white hair. He looked to be in his seventies, but still had most of his hair as it was slicked back tightly to his scalp. As the older gentleman stepped closer toward the surveillance camera, the men staring at the monitor couldn't help but to notice his luminescent blue eyes. And of course he was holding the dreadful letter in his hands. Before the footage revealed the older guy taping the note to the mounted keypad, SWAT noticed his pale, thin lips moving so he stopped the digital recorder and replayed it. SWAT's sophisticated equipment did just about everything from track movement to record in darkness; however, the cameras had no audio. Hugo and SWAT were forced to attempt to read the older man's lips. SWAT slowed the second replay down a little and both men knew exactly what words were produced. He looked directly into the camera and uttered, "Your ride is ready and waiting, sir." Then the creepy old man taped the letter over the keypad and camera. Hugo was absolutely freaked out. He stood up from his chair and began to tirade. He cried out, "What if this disgusting letter is some sort of curse? Or, what if someone *is* really out to kill me?"

SWAT abruptly interjected, "This is nothing man. Calm down and trust me. This is nothing at all. What it looks like to me is sneaky Sebastian Brody is conjuring up new ways to restrain his son."

Hugo replied, "No way man. This is just way too weird for my dad." Before Hugo stormed out of the sweaty security room, SWAT reiterated the fact that this whole event was either a prank, or the work of his sleuth-like father. He said, "No need to worry Mr. Quarterback, I'll find out who that old guy was, and I'd put a thousand bucks on it that he knows Sebastian Brody. And if you just want to kick back and relax for awhile, I'll tell the boys to keep it kind of quiet for the next few nights."

Hugo left the room but SWAT continued to study the footage from different angles in hope of catching a glimpse at a license plate or finding something that they may have overlooked. He found nothing. The aged gentleman was even careful enough to put his hearse in reverse and back all the way out of the driveway.

Hugo was on his way to his room when he purposely decided to take a pass through the kitchen. He wanted to take another glance at the awful note still sitting on the island in the center of the kitchen. He stood over it deliberating, and trying to find meaning to all of the absurdity.

CHAPTER 12

SWAT adhered to his promise. He gave the orders to Big Cane and Marinky to scale back the number of guests to just some close friends and to keep the evening's festivities low-key. Big Cane and Marinky were expecting a large blow-out and seemed highly disappointed, but they complied. The men could tell that Hugo was slightly troubled by the incident with the letter and they respected him enough to be mindful. After all, Hugo was not his usual charming and jazzed up self. He did not mingle, and isolated himself on one of the loveseats for most of the night. Marinky interrupted Hugo's moment of solitude by handing him his favorite mixed concoction. Hugo graciously accepted and guzzled the entire drink down in seconds. He slammed the stocky glass off of the table next to him hard enough to cause the full cubes of ice to clank off of the bottom of the glass several times. He then requested another. Marinky showed excitement that his friend was beginning to show evidence of vigor. The huge bodyguard even blurted, "My pleasure El Milagro. The Miracle is back baby!" Marinky mixed a second drink and handed it to his leader fulfilling his request. "Here ya' go. A couple more of these and you'll be feelin' OK." Hugo snatched the drink and said, "I'm going outside to rejuvenate."

Hugo stepped outside, opened his mouth and took in a gaping breath of the cool calm Northern California air. He then fired up a cigarette to enjoy full tranquility. He glanced upward to see the huge, bright full moon. As he peered toward the sky, he was caught off balance a little and thought to himself, "Oh my God, I'm buzzed already." He was enjoying his relaxed little cigarette break outside until his eyes caught a glimpse of that ugly mannequin across the field. The dummy was perfectly silhouetted by the moon, similar to an actor performing a soliloquy on stage. He then saw a crow swoop down from the darkness to perch on the right shoulder of the mannequin. He began to wonder if it could be the same crow that he has heard squawk annoyingly on previous nights. His eyes were fixed intently on the bird as well as the figure just waiting to hear a loud shriek. Hugo blinked to refocus and when the image became clear again he could've sworn that it had moved closer. Even though he knew deep down that the mannequin had been stationary for nearly a year, it appeared to be stepping toward him. He furiously lit another cigarette and began to huff it until the cherry amber grew to nearly an inch. It burned with intensely. He dropped the fiery cigarette as a scalding sensation penetrated his fingers and thumb. The red ash just missed his bare foot. He tried not to look at the dummy, but couldn't resist the revolting temptation. His eyes were fixated. The cool air was dense, and it prevented the smoke from rising. Through the haze he became aware that the mannequin's eyes looked different from what he had remembered. They glistened, and were slightly tinted red. Paranoid thoughts dominated his meditation ever since he had become the recipient of that grim letter. He started to think that maybe his father installed cameras in the eyes of the mannequin to view his own child's sins. He grew increasingly more nervous as the figure looked larger and then he peevishly reached for the doorknob. Before opening the door, he paused. He was the ultimate showman and he wanted to try to regain a sense of composure before entering. But, then the crow let out its deafening relentless screech. He busted through the door gasping uncontrollably with no color to his skin. All of the bodyguards rushed over to tend to their confounded employer. Big Cane tried his best to help defuse the situation with humor by saying, "What happened out there man? Did you get antiqued or something?" The star quarterback recognized that he was indeed causing a scene, and within seconds transformed his outward expression. He returned to his cool, unruffled self and the guests carried on as if never interrupted.

That same evening, a small, rare altercation took place behind the bar. Shortly after Hugo's delusional behavior, SWAT approached Marinky who had been playing the role of bartender all night long. SWAT whispered something into Marinky's ear that he must have taken offense to. Marinky retorted loudly, "No I didn't!" Something obviously ignited SWAT's temper, because he proceeded to grab Marinky by his thick neck and then pulled him into the nearby bathroom. Apparently the two giants were able to resolve their differences in the restroom because both men returned to the party wearing a smile.

Friends and onlookers speculated and debated over what the argument may have been about. Some agreed that Marinky disrespected SWAT, while others felt that SWAT was angry at his friend for serving drinks that were too strong (particularly Hugo's mixed beverage) The altercation was forgotten almost instantaneously just as Hugo's incident outside on the front porch was. No one from that night remembered such miniscule episodes, for they seemed insignificant at the time. However, if any of the guests would've just stopped partying for a second and paid attention to what was happening, they could've easily uncovered a tremendous, ungodly secret.

CHAPTER 13

The crew, as well as the star quarterback, stayed up almost all night. Hugo, in the wee hours of the morning, urged guests to accompany him on a joyride in his maroon Lamborghini. He was noticeably intoxicated, so SWAT made a substantial effort to make sure that Hugo had zero access to car keys. The huge bodyguard was also straightforward with his boss telling him that he was in no condition to drive. Marinky and Big Cane contributed to Hugo's confinement by passing word to all of the guests that if they were to get in an automobile with Hugo behind the wheel, then they would no longer be welcomed back to The Donjon. Hugo was persistent in his quest for adventure. He spent a great deal of time randomly searching through drawers and on top of tall appliances. He began to nag SWAT for a set of keys repeatedly, but then he detected that SWAT had grown perturbed and quite annoyed of his antics. So he stopped irritating everyone and finally ceased his aimless searching for car keys. He paraded one last time through all of the rooms that were still busy with convocations, and told everyone that he was going to bed. The ever so charming and irresistible quarterback really didn't get much of a response from his friends and visitors, like he had envisioned. He anticipated hugs, kisses, and women begging to accompany him, but it didn't happen. Nothing happened. It was almost as if no one had even taken notice. He was quite heated about basically being ignored *at his own house, at his own party*, but mainly about going to bed alone. Just as he turned the corner to ascend up the steps to his quarters, almost simultaneously a new guest arrived. The adorable young female was holding a set of keys in her hand as she entered. Smoothly, Hugo ushered her through the entrance, kissed her on the lips, dipped her body backward, and flawlessly swiped the young lady's keys from her hand all in one motion. The girl just assumed it was protocol, similar to as if she had worn a jacket, he would have taken it from her. The very attractive brunette woman knew nothing, so she made nothing of the matter. In fact, no one even knew Hugo left the party … that is until later.

The irrational quarterback somehow located her small compact car by pressing all of the buttons on the keychain. He decided that he would have breakfast by himself at a small diner near Nade's Malls just a few miles away. He drove hastily for a short time, and then momentarily glanced into his rearview mirror. He made the mistake of taking his eyes off the road, and when he looked ahead once again he saw a beaming set of red brake lights. Hugo Brody, the untouchable superstar, careened off the edge of the pavement and collided with a tree on a back road about a mile from his mansion. His trivial joyride ended as his head smacked the steering wheel's airbag with great force. Although he remained conscience, he did not move. He was still bracing his rigid body for he was stunned at what he had just done. He didn't see any other cars on the secluded road. "Where in the world did that car come from? What were they stopping for?" He thought. He peered out through the cracked windshield and the dense white wall of dust particles to try to get an estimate of the damage. He could clearly see that the young woman's small car was no longer drivable. However, he attempted to start the severely damaged car numerous times without success. Still feeling shocked but nearly sober, paranoid thoughts once again crept into the quarterback's head. As he sat there in the demolished car, he envisioned the police arriving, and arresting him for grand theft auto as well as driving under the influence. He thought about the police embarrassing him by making him complete a field sobriety test, which he knew deep down that he would not even come close to passing. So he decided that the only rational thing to do was to call his beloved crew of bodyguards in this moment of dire need. He rigorously felt for his cell phone in his pocket, and realized that his right shoulder, his priceless throwing arm, was having a difficult time locating it. Upon impact, the seatbelt restrained his body, but it was at the cost of his right shoulder which took the brunt of the force. He attempted again, and strained to pull the phone from his pocket. Hugo could not believe the predicament he was in. He started to search his phone's memory for SWAT's cell phone number, but right before he had a chance to hit the send button to connect the call to his enormous friend, Hugo's phone rang. The default ring tone sounded deafening as it carried throughout the woods on the old back road. The now panicked quarterback did not recognize the number, but he answered the call anyway.

The man introduced himself as Bruce Delano from the coroner's office. He told Hugo first that he was sorry to call and disturb him so early in the morning, but felt that it was imperative for him to know that his father had passed away about one hour ago due to a heart attack. Hugo dropped his phone in disbelief and it bounced off of the car's foot molding and into a thick bush. The man's voice continued its ascension from the dense shrub. He said faintly, "I am a close friend of your father's, Hugo, and I am very sorry to awaken you with such horrible news." He went on further to say, "And if you need anything you call me okay. My name is Bruce Delano. I'm an old friend of your fathers." Bruce was still barking out the telephone number at the coroner's office when Hugo opened the door of the small car and lifted himself out. He stood with both arms rested on top of the car simply refusing to believe. He didn't even notice the pain in his shoulder. He was contemplating his life, and life's purpose. He had already begun to blame himself for his father's death and the man's voice could still be heard protruding from the bushes. He closed his eyes, ignored the crash as if it was completely unobservable and felt incredible sensations of physical, as well as mental anguish. He sadly thought of his father's last requests, his eternal disapproval, and how often his only son ignored the advice. The last thing he wanted to hear from that wretched phone call was that his venerable father had passed away. He unwillingly broke down into tears. Two life altering, devastating, events had occurred nearly simultaneously, and Hugo could find no one to fault but himself. The aftermath left the one time arrogant quarterback trapped in a pit of despair.

CHAPTER 14

Hugo, fortunately, walked away from the accident. He was no longer concerned about the police getting involved. He ambulated slowly back in the direction of the Donjon thinking profoundly about his life, his current path of existence, and the choices that he has made. In somewhat of a dreamlike state, the quarterback returned to his house just as the sun began to rise.

SWAT and the boys towed the crashed car back to The Donjon, and stowed it behind the huge mansion out of plain sight. They cleaned up the crash sight as if it never even occurred, and SWAT personally informed the young brunette of the situation. The giant bodyguard compensated her $30,000 for her vehicle, and also told her that absolutely nobody can find out about what had transpired. The press, the police, nor his relatives ever heard about the wreck. It was not difficult to keep it a secret because it was so overwhelmingly overshadowed by the death of his father.

Hugo solemnly walked up the stairs to his bed. Despite being exhausted, Hugo Brody could not get comfortable enough to fall asleep. His slightly foggy brain was still trying process all that had occurred. He became increasingly aware of the fact that he needed to make some changes in his life real soon, or his funeral would soon follow his father's. Only after convincing himself that he would alter his lifestyle, did he finally sleep.

Hugo did not sleep for long as he was awakened by a vivid, yet horrific, nightmare. His pillow was freezing cold, but soaked. He dreamt of a situation during a game where he dropped back to throw a pass, and then he collapsed on the field and died. What he remembered most about the terrible dream was that he did not die immediately. He lay on his back in the middle of the football field gasping for air and writhing just long enough to notice the hundreds of thousands of fans that oddly continued to cheer. Hugo basically remained in his bed for the rest of that day, though he failed to sink again into a sound slumber. He used the bathroom twice, and even drank the water from the bathroom sink just so he wouldn't have to go downstairs.

Hugo ignored most of the phone calls from friends and relatives, but SWAT took messages for him. SWAT informed his increasingly detached leader that the remnants of his family were gathering at Sebastian's house already, and that the funeral will be carried out tomorrow afternoon.

Only SWAT and Hugo left for the funeral later on that night. Big Cane and Marinky stayed back at The Donjon. The ride seemed like an eternity for both men. Hugo dozed off in the plush, ultra reclined passenger seat about midway through the journey. He was suddenly awakened once again after a short time by the same dream where he had dropped back to throw a pass, and then collapsed. The fans carried on joyfully just as they had in his prior disturbance. The only difference with this episode was the fact that Hugo felt as if he was anticipating his fall in this dream. He fought tirelessly to get back up onto his feet, but his torso was completely numb and unresponsive.

SWAT slowed down the car a little to ask his buddy if he was alright. The huge guard looked over and noticed that his boss was sweating excessively. He said nervously, "Hugo, man, are you okay? Who were you fightin' in that dream anyway? Your body was all stiff, and you were grunting and stuff."

Hugo answered, "I think I was fighting death." SWAT looked surprised, and had attempted to abate his friend by expressing some kind, reassuring words. He could tell that Hugo was bothered so he quickly reverted back to his silence. Hugo *was* bothered by the dream. In fact, he was beginning to get agitated by the grisly nightmare, but he was also starting to get worried. He feared that these terrible dreams will linger on, but he feared most that he may be witnessing his own fate through some prophetic vision.

Soon the irritable quarterback, who struggled strenuously to focus and function on very little sleep, as well as his concerned large sidekick, arrived at Sebastian Brody's house. Once there, the two men were greeted and consoled by grieving friends and relatives. They split up and began to visit individually with those present. To the crowd of mourners, Hugo looked completely different from when they had last seen him. It was difficult for some to even recognize the great quarterback. He looked confused, deeply saddened and quite fatigued. He struggled to keep his posture from anything but constant slouching. His speech was slow but terse. His physical appearance had strikingly deteriorated. He was incredibly pale, unshaved, and his eyes were extraordinarily red and swollen. He had a look on his face like he questioned whether or not he should even be there. Yet he made a consistent effort to confer with most of the people present.

Hugo rested, but barely slept once again. He ate a little in the morning and actually started to feel a little better. The few hours after breakfast passed by quickly and it was time for the initial sermon and first showing. There was an enormous turnout. The funeral home was congested. It was customary that immediate family viewed the corpse, as well as, paid their respects first. Hugo stepped close to the coffin and began his apologetic homage in front of hundreds of grief stricken men and women. He thought to himself, "I love you, dad. I'm sorry for not listening to you. I will become a better person, I promise." A tear fell from his bloodshot eye. "This is so hard," he thought. "I feel partially responsible dad," he thought internally. Then the sorrowful son moved closer to the coffin and stretched out his hand to touch his father's. Both eyes filled to capacity, and tears began sliding down his pallid cheeks. Just before his trembling hand made contact with the deceased, Sebastian Brody's upper torso lifted up from the underpinning of the casket. He looked his son directly in the eye and pointed to him. Sebastian's mouth began to gape open as if he had something profound to say. Hugo couldn't find any oxygen as he stared in awe. His eyebrows, mouth and face twisted as he turned and ran out of the funeral home like he was being chased by a herd of stampeding bulls. He practically flattened two small children who had crossed into his path. All of the faces of those who were in attendance exhibited the same shocked, deplorable expression. No one amongst the congregation of mourners knew the cause of Hugo's violent, hysterical exit. SWAT scurried after him only to find his frightened manager lying on his back in the grass near his vehicle. Hugo was staring vacantly toward the gloomy gray sky covered in perspiration. SWAT, totally oblivious to what could have caused such an insane reaction, picked up his inoperative pal and placed him in the passenger's seat. He basically wanted to help extinguish the situation, and thought of how the repercussions might destroy his boss's image.

The big guy said to Hugo, "Let's get out of here, man. What do you think?" Hugo did not respond verbally, but looked at SWAT and nodded in an up and down motion. They were going back home.

The two traveled for some distance before SWAT finally built up enough courage to ask his friend what had happened. He knew Hugo was extremely distressed and he did not want to push him to the brink of another nervous breakdown right there in the passenger seat.

In a manner about as sensitive as a giant bodyguard could be, SWAT said, "What happened back there man? Are you goin' crazy or something?"

Hugo replied, "I think I'm gonna die soon." SWAT was actually more surprised by the fact that Hugo responded, rather than his actual words. Hugo continued, "I've been hallucinating or having some sort of visions over the last few months. I've been seeing things, weird things, ever since we found that damn note."

"You are the most paranoid person I've ever met El Milagro," SWAT interjected. He always tried to cheer his boss up during low times.

Hugo continued to vent, "I've been having that reoccurring dream all of the time. I swear someone else besides my father has been sneaking around the house, and whoever it is may be trying to kill me. I even fired my barber of ten years last week because he slipped with his scissors too close to my neck. I mean, SWAT, you're like the only guy I can trust. I've noticed that I have been blinking longer too. I'm tellin' you man, either I'm gonna' die soon, or I'm gonna end up in somebody's basement chained to the wall or something."

SWAT stopped his manager's blathering momentarily and said, "You need therapy, man. You are clearly out of your mind. What caused you to freak out at your own father's funeral?"

Hugo said, "Forget it. You won't believe me anyway."

SWAT replied, "Come on now, I'm listening to you."

Hugo looked over at him with the most confused of all countenances and said, "He pointed at me and was about to say something." The steering wheel jerked a little and the vehicle snapped slightly to the left side of the road.

SWAT said, "You're kiddin' me right?"

"No man, I wish I was. My father opened his eyes, looked

straight into mine, and pointed at me like he was about to scold me for something," Hugo stated.

SWAT said, "We gotta get you some help man. I'm serious. The season starts in a couple of days!" The conversation ended with Hugo conceding, "I killed my own father, man."

CHAPTER 15

(THE RECEDING SEER)

Hugo cracked his window and lit a cigarette. Up to this point he had only smoked when he drank. SWAT was well aware that his buddy was deeply troubled by the passing of his father, but thought that it was a little unusual none the less. The two men were only about an hour and a half away from home when a faint little secondary sign along the roadway caught the quarterback's attention. Hugo flicked his cigarette out of the small crack in the window and said, "Get off here! Pull off here!" His mammoth comrade obeyed his sudden request and veered off of the main road, mostly just because he was stunned from the break in silence. Hugo said, "I won't do therapy. I just need to know if I'm going to collapse in the middle of a game. I need to know if I'm going to die soon."

The barely noticeable sign near the road was an advertisement for a local psychic named Lady Garfold. SWAT couldn't believe he was about to take part in such nonsense, because he knew that these supposed fortune tellers were a complete waste of time and money. Nevertheless, the skeptic and the believer pulled into the driveway of a small tattered mobile home. It was reassuring to both men that there were plenty of signs to the psychic's quarters so the place must have obviously had *some* cliental.

The men walked up three steps onto the dilapidated front porch and were about an arm's length away from ringing the doorbell, when they heard Lady Garfold say, "Please come in." Her voice was sweet, and she sounded quite young for a psychic. Both men entered and immediately were told to sit on the couch. They were equally amazed at the fact that the couch and a circular coffee table were basically the extent of the furnishings in the place. The pair were thoroughly out of their element.

Lady Garfold soon entered the room dragging an old wooden chair behind her. She was indeed young, and had a nice athletic build, but was almost completely bald on the top of her head. Despite her patterned baldness, she had long black hair that streamed down her back. The seer sat down directly across from Hugo and took her time to study him. Hugo returned the gaze in wonder, and was even a little curious as to whether or not she recognized him as a celebrity. She pointed to SWAT and asked, "Is he going to stay for this session?" She spoke quickly and Hugo felt compelled to nod yes repeatedly, but he also mentioned that the big guy must stay in the room.

The quarterback declared, "He is my bodyguard ma'm and never leaves my side."

Lady Garfold discreetly rolled her eyes and said, "Okay

then let us begin. Here are your instructions. If you do not concentrate, your six hundred dollar session will be a waste of your own time and money. Secondly, you must look me directly in the eyes when asking a question. Third, your right palm must be pressed against the top of my head while asking a question. And lastly, you are permitted to ask only three questions. Do you agree with the instructions that I have set forth?" Hugo, somewhat astounded, shook his head in understanding.

The bizarre seer reached into her front pocket, pulled out a tiny hourglass, and flipped it over. She said, "Alright, go. You have ten minutes."

Hugo cautiously stood up and placed his hand firmly to the bald spot atop Lady Garfold's head. He looked her dead in the eye and asked, "Am I going to die while dropping back to throw a pass in front of one hundred thousand people?" The fortune teller's eyes sort of rolled back into her head so that the men could only see the whites. She was taking an extraordinary length of time to respond. It was really awkward for Hugo because he was just standing there with his hand on the top of some unfamiliar woman's bare scalp.

She emphasized, "Keep your palm firmly pressed and focus. It's coming to me." Hugo began to think this was a scam. He was about one second from removing his sweaty palm and leaving when he heard the soothsayer's voice. Her speech was different compared to how nice it sounded upon first arrival. She said to Hugo Brody in a deeper tone, "No, you will not die on football field." She sounded similar to how a Native American would be depicted in old movies or on television. Hugo was relieved for a brief moment, however, now his curiosity was stimulated as to how or when he would perish.   The gifted athlete once again secured his moist palm to the seer's hairless head. As he regained full concentration, he quickly decided that the more appropriate and useful question to ask next would be *when* he was going to die. The fortune teller's eyes infolded and once again beamed as white as two large cotton balls. She took even longer to reply to his second question. She uttered, "Wait, it is coming to me. It is coming to me," several times. And then in that same untamed, indigenous voice, she claimed, "You will pass on when all holes are filled in."

Hugo gave the seer a look of disgust and replied loudly, "I wanted to know when! That doesn't tell me a date or time or anything." Lady Garfold said nothing in response to Hugo's comments. She simply pointed to the hourglass, sat, and waited patiently for the third question. Hugo, obviously riled, struggled to recapture his focus until he saw that there was very little sand left and that it was beginning to pass through the narrow part of the tube. He rushed to come up with a final question and impetuously blurted out, "Who is trying to kill me?"

The seer hesitated for a few seconds and said, "I have no name, but I see face of dangerous man to you. He is bitter old white man with large moustache and silver glasses." Just then her dialect reverted to the same kind voice that had greeted the two men earlier at the door. Her brown eyes positioned themselves correctly in the sockets as she chimed, "Your session is over. Thank you."

Hugo removed his hand, and looked over at SWAT who had

been lounging comfortably on the couch. The shocked superstar told his bodyguard, "See, I knew someone was out to get me. Now you know who to protect me from. Some bitter old white guy with a big moustache and glasses."

SWAT replied cynically, "Ya, ya and you believe everything this woman tells you. Come on Mr. Brody; let me escort you to your car. You are so gullible sometimes." Hugo handed Lady Garfold the six hundred dollars and followed his protection closer than ever out to his vehicle.

Once Hugo had safely returned to the car, he instantly began to reflect on his consultation with the seer. First he brooded over the physical features of the man that Lady Garfold had warned him about. He was frustrated because he didn't know that many older people. And he certainly couldn't recognize anyone in his memory bank that fit the description of someone with a large moustache and eyeglasses. Even when he thought about some of his dad's friends, or people that he may have betrayed at some point in his life, his mind drew a blank. It wasn't that he had doubted the profound psychic's prediction, but he honestly could not envision a man resembling the given depiction.

As for the answer he was given to his second question, Hugo was not sure at all about what to make of it. He was thinking it could possibly be interpreted as to when all of the planet's landfills are filled to capacity. Or, it might be related to some sort of accident that takes place later on in life. Either way it didn't sound anywhere near as awful as dropping back to throw a pass and collapsing in front of thousands of his fans. Needless to say, the star quarterback viewed this specific prediction as much too vague to take serious. He also concluded that perhaps it may be illegal for a fortune teller to give an exact date or time that one would die.

He would contemplate over the meaning of the statements made by the fortune teller for the entire ride home, but never questioned their validity. SWAT repeatedly called Hugo naive and pondered over whether or not he should seek some assistance that is not moronic for his associate. Hugo's sixth full season in the National Football League was about to begin. He was to report to training camp in just two days, but to the volatile superstar, that was the least of his worries.

CHAPTER 16

Hugo's flight for training camp in Arizona was scheduled to leave in thirty-six hours. His friends hated to see him wake up the next morning still severely depressed and in complete disarray. Big Cane, Marinky, and SWAT secretly conglomerated to brainstorm a plan to help their leader forget about his most recent, woefully unfortunate, events. Marinky suggested that he would organize an evening viewing of Hugo's past Super Bowl highlights to help get his competitive juices flowing once again in anticipation for the upcoming season.

Big Cane mentioned, "If anything was gonna boost his morale, it would be a 'ladies only' party," as he followed his statement with a wink.

SWAT added, "Let's take it one step further, and invite the most obsessed fans that I have been receiving messages from for the past few years. These desperate MOF's would cater to poor

Hugo all night long." SWAT mischievously rubbed his hands together. "They would certainly make sure he enjoyed himself." It was determined that they should get their leader's permission before inviting the MOF's. Marinky and Big Cane immediately began editing Super Bowl footage to compile a highlight film. Marinky also set up the projector and the white screen in the enormous living room. SWAT approached Hugo with what he considered a once in a lifetime opportunity. SWAT said to his employer, "You won't go to counseling, so me and the crew had to take matters into our own hands. Your last free night for a very long time will be one that you will never forget. We have decided to ask for your permission to invite the female MOF's over tonight. You deserve to be pampered and you desperately are in need of a little cheering up."

Hugo said, "I don't know man, I thought you said that some of these ladies could be dangerous."

SWAT replied, "Well, that's what you pay us for. We must protect Hugo "El Milagro" Brody. Come on, just say yes, man. You need this before training camp begins, and I know it will be a blast!" SWAT always knew how to push the right buttons when it came to his boss. Hugo agreed that it would be fun, and that he was in need of a mental cleansing. After the crash, his own father's death that he had taken full responsibility for, and all of the bad omens, Hugo incredulously gave his friend SWAT the consent to go forth with the plans. His approval of the MOF party was testament that the quarterback's judgment was seriously unclear and unstable at that time. It also proved to be the most devastating and detrimental of all of his mistakes.

SWAT intensively sent messages and called phone numbers to close to thirty of the ladies he so kindly dubbed the "most obsessed fans." His messages consisted of a personal invitation (by name), directions to The Donjon, a starting time of 8:00 p.m., and an apology to those who could not attend because of the just a half day's notice for travel time. SWAT also strongly mandated that they were not to bring any male friends with them. SWAT was fully aware of the short notice, but he was confident that these were the types of ladies who would drop everything to spend a night with Hugo. These women were the MOF's, and he was positive that some would turn out.

The men were drinking and swapping football stories while watching the Chargers beat up on the Seattle Seahawks on the Super Bowl highlight film when, at 7:56pm, the buzzer on the main gate sounded. SWAT sprung to his size eighteens, rushed excitedly to see the camera and shouted, "Fellas, our first MOF has arrived." The men were anxious, and fully anticipated a fun filled night of unexpected disorder. Stephanie was the first to arrive. She entered with lengthy catwalk strides wearing a long dark jacket, but amorously slipped it off from the shoulders and smiled once she had proceeded through the doorway. The men were instantly entertained and aroused because underneath the coat was just a bright yellow skimpy bikini. The men whistled and cheered as they followed her incredible, tan body. As soon as the guys started to get passed the initial chitchat with Stephanie, the second MOF appeared, Heather. Heather took a last minute direct flight all the way from Louisiana to join the festivities. She had a really cute face, but SWAT purposely mispronounced her name when he introduced her to Marinky, calling her Heifer. She was fairly large, but the men appreciated her effort to make it to the party especially after travelling such a great distance.

After another round of cocktails, the third MOF arrived. Her name was Erica and the crew immediately thanked SWAT for inviting her as she entered. Erica was an amazing beauty who could've easily been a model. She was tall, enhanced even more by her long heels, and had marvelous light blonde hair. Following her was Kaitlyn. Kaitlyn was very nice looking, but the men weren't certain of her age. They asked her how old she was numerous times, but she refused to divulge the information. Eventually SWAT asked to see her driver's license because she truly did look under the age of eighteen. She was reluctant to show them her identification, and was even somewhat agitated by all of the scrutiny. It wasn't until the huge bodyguards threatened to make her leave that she handed over the driver's license. It revealed that she was twenty years old. The crew was slightly concerned because she did not meet the legal drinking age requirement, but Big Cane pointed out the fact that it probably hasn't been the first time an underage girl has partied in The Donjon. So unfortunately Kaitlyn was permitted to stay.

During the whole issue with the driver's license, a fifth MOF walked through the main door. Her name was Isabel, and she spoke with a Latin accent. She was also unbelievably alluring, however she remained much more reserved in comparison to the other girls. The next two MOF's walked in together, and heads turned instantaneously. The two voluptuous women were wearing scant police uniforms, and were the most strikingly gorgeous set of identical twins that the men had ever laid eyes on. Their shiny little silver nametags read Lucy and Lisa. Hugo and his crew were definitely starting to enjoy the scenery after the first seven had arrived, and were having a great time with all of the ladies. Samantha was the eighth MOF to enter the wild party, and it was around 9:20pm. She was a lively, seductive little sprite. The temptress bounced from man to man groping and fondling them while she shared her ideas about intimacies and fantasies. Haley was ninth at about 10:00 p.m., and showed up overly dressed in an elegant gown. Unfortunately, by the time she had arrived, Hugo and the crew had started to feel the effects of the alcohol and were jocundly making comments about the young woman's choice of clothing. Haley forced Marinky to redesign her exquisite dress with a pair of scissors to make it more suitable. She clearly embraced the attention, even if some of it was intended to be negative. The men were beginning to get more rambunctious and a little more flirtatious with all of the girls when the stunning India arrived as the number ten MOF. She was another ravishing young lady who could easily qualify as a magazine or runway model. She arrived late, but quickly caught up by doing three shots of tequila just minutes after her entry. The Donjon was as boisterous as it had been in its earliest days of existence. Hugo and the crew had decided that having ten out of the close to thirty that were invited show up for their party on such short notice was definitely a laudable amount. They were also quite surprised by how nice all of the girls were.

The men really started to target certain girls because it was after midnight and they were fairly certain that only the ten

MOF's present were coming. SWAT was focused on the dynamite twins, Lisa and Lucy. He had both of their badges pinned to the front of his tight fitting shirt. Marinky was quite fond of the beautiful Erica, and followed her around constantly like a clingy toddler. Big Cane and India seemed to connect from the start as they continued to down shots of tequila together. Hugo pursued several MOF's and repeated the process. Neither his expectations, nor his aspirations for finding the perfect partner were even close to measuring up to his standards. He had a difficult time trying to make a connection with any of the girls. He was disappointed because he felt like he was going to have to *settle* on a companion for his final night of freedom. He started spending more time on the couch watching himself throw touchdowns on the large opaque projector screen, and rapidly imbibing. That is, until a little after 1:00am when the eleventh MOF guest made her arrival.

Hugo was waiting on another cocktail and he just happened to notice headlights approaching. He stood up a little too sudden in excitement for he nearly lost his balance and had gone tumbling forward. Hugo snatched his beverage from the evening's bartender, Big Cane, and waited for the buzzing sound on the security gate. Hugo struggled to find the correct button to enable her vehicle to pass through the massive gate. Then, he waited impatiently by the front door. He was feeling quite a buzz from the booze, but tried to act extra suave as he instantly greeted her. She was very nice looking and of course Hugo made her out to be even more appealing based on what he had already known about his other female options. She had short brown hair held up by two ponytails, and Hugo really loved her sporty combination of the long tube socks and short gym shorts. Even though the star quarterback was beginning to feel intoxicated, he thought that he had seen the attractive female before somewhere or some place. He inquired, "Do I know you? You look so familiar. What's your name?"

She replied, "My name is Monica, Monica Resser. And we did meet once a long time ago in college. In fact, we almost hooked up one night. But I'm fairly certain that you don't remember that."

Hugo, stumbling over his words uttered, "No, I re-cood-nize you from somewhere. I just doanmember." He was squinting, and his slurring and babbling was barely understood.

SWAT temporarily left the sultry twins to rush over to assist his boss. The big bodyguard said unsettlingly, "Hugo, you know I'm supposed to grant entrance. You pay me to monitor these situations and to protect you. I guess I can forgive you this time El Milagro, but don't let it happen again." Both men welcomed her, and ushered over to the bar where all three received ice cold drinks. Hugo attempted to tell his large friend exactly who the young woman was, but his incoherent mumbling was getting too severe. She was walking around and mingling with guests as Hugo continued to try to be witty. She stopped to talk to Heather who was sitting on a sofa by herself. Like a trained dog, Hugo sat right beside her as she conversed with one of the more lonely girls in attendance. The elite quarterback was closely admiring Monica's straight brown hair to the point were he even began petting it. She appreciated the attention that she was receiving from the man whom she admired, even though she could plainly see that he was inebriated. Monica even frivolously caressed Hugo's oily locks to show that she was willing to put up with his foolish behavior.

As time passed and it got much later, relationships formed, couples disappeared, and guests made their way upstairs to go to their bedrooms for the night. Only a few singles were awake, still holding on for the slim chance that they might fulfill their dream to have one night with the great Hugo Brody. Hugo was completely incapacitated and had difficulty with the most basic functioning, but Monica managed to tolerate his indecency. Soon, everyone except Hugo and the most obsessed fan of all time, Monica Resser, were the only two still awake. They were harmlessly kissing and petting on the sofa when Hugo zoomed in and tried to pull down her snug shorts. He was playfully charming in his attempts to romance her at first. But then after his advances were denied several times, Hugo started to get aggressive. She suggested that he go upstairs and get some sleep. Monica, who had returned the teasing and flirting all night, suddenly wanted nothing to do with him and it further fueled his forcefulness. He grabbed and squeezed one of her wrists sharply. She was so appalled and disgusted with the man that she had once adored that she pushed his arm away and attempted to evacuate. A belligerent, lewd version of the great Hugo Brody would not accept "no" for an answer, and he certainly wasn't going to let her leave. She grabbed her car keys out of her pocket and tried desperately to escape through the door in which she had originally entered through. He relentlessly chased his prey toward the front door and caught her from behind in the middle of the kitchen. As he grabbed the young lady by the back of her shirt near the waistline, her legs flew back behind her as her momentum carried her upper torso forward. The top of her forehead violently struck the edge of the center island. Monica's body went limp as she blacked out. Hugo erupted with a demented, sadistic laughter while he held her wilted frame. Hugo used his pure strength to lift the unconscious Monica Resser up onto the island where the men usually gather to eat breakfast. He positioned her on her back. Ironically, her motionless body lay directly upon the mysterious letter that Hugo had once conceived to be a bad omen. In fact, a small amount of blood had oozed onto the strange list of dead celebrities just before Hugo stripped her of her clothes. He buried all of her clothes in the bottom of the kitchen trash can, except for her long white gym socks, which he miraculously managed to stuff both tightly into her mouth, partially down her throat. The tragic and gruesome rape that took place that night in the kitchen is far too graphic to describe for the intended purpose of this story. It was a malicious, wretched, and deviant act. It was a scene that could have been described as borderline necrophilia, but what made it even worse was the fact that it had been grotesquely gradual. The once proud quarterback generously had his way with the unresponsive young lady over quite a long period of time. The meticulous deviate positioned her arms and legs for her; otherwise there was no volitional movement except for a path of blood that trickled across her lovely forehead. As if the rape wasn't brutal enough, when Hugo was finished with her, he placed her abused body underneath the sink in its spacious cabinetry. To make sure she did not escape, Hugo located some multi-purpose plastic zip ties in the utility drawer nearby and attached one around her feet. He also lassoed one around both wrists, tightly fastening them to the pipes and interior plumbing. Despite a rather efficient cleanup effort, Hugo remained hazy and unclear. His face was inexpressive, and his eyes wandered without focus or devotion similarly to a blind man's. He could not distinctly decipher between which world he was present. At times, the quarterback operated carefully and clear, and then would return to his hallucinatory dreamlike stupor.

After wiping up a petty sum of blood then burying the rag in the bottom of the trash can, Hugo staggered his way up the steps and went into what he thought was his own bedroom. He fell as he opened the door and landed on his stomach. He was snoring loudly before his face even made contact with the gentle rug. He slept there on the floor for only a few minutes when Big Cane awakened him. Cane said repeatedly, "Hugo, wake up man. You're in *my* room. Go to your own bed." Hugo finally did respond to Big Cane's requisition, and he looked around through tiny slits to attempt to see what was going on. He knew he was in the wrong room because there was a bright florescent light coming from some sort of fish tank or terrarium, and Hugo kept his bedroom as dark as the deep sea. After he had struggled to climb onto his feet, he heard the loud croaking of several toads. He used a combination of his shoulder and the hallway wall to propel his sloppy somnambulistic strides into the correct chamber. He was fortunate to find his mattress in his condition. He fell into a deep sleep once again without even recollecting the barbaric act of rape. He didn't even remember sleeping on the floor in Big Cane's room, or the grumbling toads.

CHAPTER 17

The majority of the female attendees from the previous night's get together had all departed early in the morning with the exception of those girls who were linked to the great men of The Donjon. The crew, as well as their boss, slept through the entire day only abandoning the comfort of their beds out of necessity for a drink, or to use the bathroom. By midday, all of the MOF's had vacated The Donjon. The girls left completely unaware of Hugo's despicable deed. The crew, who methodically percolated their way downstairs one by one in the evening hours, was also absolutely oblivious to their leader's morbid endeavor. Hugo began to stir shortly after. As he awakened, astonishingly, he did not recall a single event from the preceding night. The quarterback made a number of excursions through the kitchen and even stopped for a drink out of the refrigerator a couple of times. Yet nothing evoked any type of recollection or feeling.

The men stayed up for awhile hardly speaking. They mostly just began to pack and prepare for their early morning flight to Arizona to the Chargers training camp facilities, and then they all returned to their sleeping quarters once again.

Hugo and the crew all managed to awake in time to get to the airport, but were short on time. Just before rushing to leave The Donjon for a little over a month of training camp, all four men briefly met in the kitchen for coffee and muffins. This was when Monica Resser awakened from her unconscious state, only to hear Hugo's incessant complaining, and SWAT's vulgarity as he barked out orders. The captive MOF noticed immediately that her hands and feet were bound and panicked at the thought of not being able to move. She was engulfed in the darkness, with very little breathing space, and could only inhale through her nostrils. Then she heard SWAT say, "Alright boys, if everything is packed, let's go." She kicked furiously, punched with every drop of energy, and tried desperately to call out to someone for help. No one could hear her, for her obstruction was a pair of long tube socks compressed halfway down her esophagus. She couldn't believe that this was how she was going to die. Raped, naked, and left for dead under a kitchen sink, all while the dirty miscreant goes off to play football for all of his fans. She could not, and would not accept it. She kicked and screamed harder and harder. She made both wrists bleed from struggling. She was completely exasperated, and needed much more oxygen than what the nasal cavity could provide, so she stopped. She began to calm herself. As she listened closely, she heard a remote beeping noise over her intense breathing and assumed SWAT was setting the security alarm. She hastily attempted once again to gain SWAT's attention. She also tried to no avail to tear the homemade gag from her mouth. The door slammed abruptly separating the hostage from all sound, and all hope.

Shortly after the men abandoned her, she somehow maneuvered her hands close enough to her head and pulled the socks from her mouth. She felt like she could breathe now, and if anyone should enter the house hereafter, she could at the very least yell for help and be heard. She knew that her only chance for survival depended gravely on her ability to remain rational, so she continued to work on calming herself. She had had to urinate since awakening from her comatose, but she was severely confined. She knew that she would feel less anxiety if she would just let it go, so she did. The warmth momentarily felt pleasant, but the brief spell lasted just seconds as her nude contorted body had to grow accustomed to a relentless bitter chill.

One full week had passed and her environment underneath the kitchen sink seemed darker and damper than The Middle Passage. Days and nights had passed without her being able to tell the difference. She had to overcome the coldness as well as the mordant stench of urine. She was surviving and enduring with the hope of chewing through the thick plastic. Even though it required a strenuous neck stretch, she had nearly chewed through the plastic zip tie holding her wrists in place. She was famished and realized that she would soon die of dehydration or starvation. Monica Resser quenched her thirst and hunger by busting open the only plastic pipe directly above her head which came from the garbage disposal. As the pipe burst, with her head bleeding in a fresh area, she opened her mouth widely and accepted all of the waste that had accumulated in that particular pipe. She pretended that the moist sludge was butter. She consumed every last drop and was certain that most of remnants would eventually make her ill, but it was a chance that she had to take. She figured that it would at least provide enough energy and nourishment to allow her time to finish gnawing through the zip tie on her tightly bound wrists. After digesting the vile remains, she sat there covered in filth, blood and urine contemplating her next move. Survival became her only desire. Her front teeth had worn and deteriorated from biting and sawing on the tough plastic, however, she had not heard a single sound outside of her confinement since the crew left for training camp, so she decided that continuing to gnaw was her only option.

Finally, after strenuously eroding her teeth, she forged through the resilient synthetic and plunged through the heavy oak cabinet doors. Her cold flesh smacked off of the ceramic kitchen tiles. Despite a sudden sensation of joy, the sunlight surging through the kitchen windows scorched her eyes. It had been close to three weeks since she had last seen light. Her muscle rigidity matched the flexibility of the oaken cabinets that had once imprisoned her. One million thoughts raced through her brain, but going upstairs to get some clothes or looking for her own car keys didn't even cross her mind. She located a knife through the tiny slits created by her eyelids and quickly freed her feet and legs. She gathered her weak and tattered body, and without hesitation, hysterically ran through the main door of the house. She was aware that she may have triggered the alarm, but her stiffened muscles inhibited her from the fast escape which she had envisioned and desired. She glanced back toward the house for she heard another disturbance. Her eyes witnessed a large metal door on the basement of The Donjon had begun to open. She forced herself to go faster but the atrophy prevented. Her weak body collapsed, and she peeked over her shoulder to see two roving robots advancing toward her. She stood up and relentlessly darted toward the gate. The C-Robs triumphed through the terrain and had gained significant ground after her fall. They were close enough to Monica that she could sense their glowing red visors without even taking a glimpse to her rear. She was close enough to begin reaching for the gate to pull herself up and over, when a sharp pain ignited through the vertebrate of her lower back all the way down to her toes like a lit fuse. She didn't know what it was, nor did she care. Monica Resser had determined the moment she woke up under the kitchen sink that nothing would stop her from fleeing. She craved the day that she would one day destroy her assailant with vengeful pleasure. She grasped the iron bars of the main gate as high as her arms could reach to get out of that evil place. The numbness in her legs prevented any type of control whatsoever and she could not use them to help give her a boost. Her legs were paralyzed. She pulled and strained to elevate her mangled body just out of the reach of SWAT's two roaming security robots. Both C-Robs, just a few feet away from the gate, reached upward desperately to clench one of the former MOF's dangling, wavering legs. She climbed hand over hand using every shred of strength and soon reached the top of the tall gate. Then she heard a discreet puff of air and instantly felt a familiar agonizingly painful sting near the back of her neck.   The widespread throbbing and a feeling of being burned or torched was the last thing she experienced as the front side of her body collided with the Earth from ten feet above.

CHAPTER 18

Monica was fortunate enough to land just out of view, and out of reach of the roving "conscienceless robots." Ironically, it was all of SWAT's elaborate security cameras, devices and keypads that completely obstructed the robot's vision. They scurried about the grounds searching for the perpetrator aimlessly, but were unable to detect any movement.

Monica awakened to the sound of sirens approaching as the sun was beginning to set behind the expansive mansion. She was shocked, and in utter disbelief that she was still alive. First, she looked at the flat ground where her face had left an imprint. Her fingers gently touched her nose, but the soreness drove her hand away. Then she reached to feel the back of her neck, where she made contact with a small tranquilizer dart. She attempted to pull it out gingerly but was suffering more discomfort, so she tore it from her skin furiously. She did the same to the tiny arrow embedded in her lower back. She was badly bruised, but regained a full range of motion in all extremities. The only bone that she felt may have been broken was her nose.

The young woman, who had been knocked unconscious, chased, bruised, raped and left for dead, had escaped. Her story of survival gave her a renewed sense of strength as she walked briskly into the darkening forest. She chose the forest over the driveway and the main road essentially to hide from police, and to cover her haggard body. As vehicles approached, she chose to hide behind large timbers and decided against stopping anyone to ask for help because she remembered on her travels that there was a small gas station several miles away. She knew that she could make it on foot, and it would be safer there. After all, now she trusted nearly no one, including the police who are probably Hugo's biggest fans. Monica had decided shortly after her heroic escape that she would handle the man who had assaulted her, taken everything from her, and left her to die, all on her own.

She plotted and marched on diligently but her exposed feet were begging for a smoother surface so she walked closer to the side of the road. She carefully watched for headlights and dodged each vehicle by hiding in the woods. Automobiles were becoming more frequent, so she knew that she was getting closer to the service station near the highway exit. Soon she saw the bright sign in the sky with two giant wings on it. She instantly made the gratifying symbolic connection to that of an angel, the way its wings had illuminated the surrounding sky. As she approached the entrance, she was cognizant of her appearance, and was worried as to how the clerk might overreact. She decided that a calm, relaxed approach would be her best bet. She most certainly did not want the authorities immediately involved. She rehearsed, "No, I'm alright. Honest, I just need to use your restroom to get cleaned up a little that's all." She limped through the entrance on her gauged sore feet and the attendant alertly glanced toward her. The young man looked as if his head were about to explode. His eyes resembled two half dollars, and the skin on his scalp stretched tightly to pull back his ears. She forced a playful grin and announced graciously, "Don't worry, I'm okay. I know I look bad, but just give me a chance to get cleaned up in the restroom. It's not nearly as awful as it looks."

The male clerk looked young enough to still be in high school, and there were no customers. With a trembling voice he asked, "Do you want me to call the police?"

Monica nodded and responded, "No, I am going to get some legal advice first, but thanks anyway. Do you have any clothes I can wear?" She was poised and quite swank despite standing before the employee hardly resembling life and naked. The young man was beyond nervous as he flustered about. He agreed to help look for some clothes for her.

Monica hobbled into the dual sex bathroom. It was revoltingly foul and filthy, but she didn't seem to notice. She turned on the cold water first and stuck her mouth under the faucet. She guzzled the cool clean water enthusiastically until she no longer had the urge to consume. She softly opened the door just enough so she could take a peek at the clerk. She was a little relieved to see him continue his search for some articles of clothing. She pulled the door closed, turned off the cold water, and switched it to warm.

She washed her face gently with the lukewarm water, and looked into the mirror for the first time. She was taken back by her own reflection. That couldn't be her weary face, she thought. Her nose was crooked and badly broken, she had a deep gash near the top of her forehead with dried black blood still clumped around the wound, her cheeks looked like they could be swallowed, and both of her eyes dawned glossy red crystalline tints accentuated by cheek-long streams of dried black eyeliner. She felt pressed to cry, but thought of her tormentor and instead generated more hate. She scoured at the eyeliner, as well as the area around the laceration on her head until it appeared clean. She also rinsed the abrasions on her wrists thoroughly, and cleaned her vaginal area with more than enough soap. She exited the restroom and the cashier said, "Ma'm, I couldn't find any clothes for you in here, but there might be some next door in the servicing garage. You can check in there if you'd like. He looked disappointed, but donned an anxious frown. I'd go look myself, but I'm not allowed to leave the store unattended."

Monica replied, "That's alright, do you have a phone I could use?" He handed the distressed woman his cell phone from his pocket, and she promptly called her father to come and pick her up. Before she returned the phone to the clerk, she praised his generosity, and then checked the last call he had made, just to make sure he didn't cross her. She proceeded through the door to the service area where she found a dirty old mechanic's shirt that reeked of gasoline and some gloves to help cover up her wrists. She waited in the garage and peered through one of the tiny windows every time she heard a car pull into the station. As she waited, the abused woman planned her new vengeful objective.

Monica's father soon arrived and he watched his daughter limp as if shackled toward his automobile. He was shocked and saddened to see her in such poor condition. He asked if she wanted him to drive her to the nearest hospital, and she adamantly rejected as she plopped down into the passenger seat. He was extraordinarily understanding for a man who could not make contact with his daughter after several weeks and had just observed her struggle to walk over to his vehicle. She asked, "Did you call the police?

He replied, "No, but I was worried sick about you. I want to hear the whole story. Are you sure you're alright?" Monica reassured her father that she was okay, and she reinforced that notifying the police was not an option. Monica Resser retold the disturbing events to the best of her memory. Revisiting the past experience was appalling to her father, but the recollection made his young daughter tremble as the nightmarish details expelled from between her dry chapped lips.

After discussing the unfortunate series of events, Monica's father became infuriated by the vile act of rape. He was sickened by the disaster and felt compelled to resolve the dilemma himself. He suggested that they should go straight to the police, but Monica quickly rejected his request once again. He grew even more livid. He said in rage, "But we could get the best legal team that money could buy! That dirty rapist Hugo Brody will fry!" He readjusted his hands, tightening his grip on the steering wheel.

Monica stared out the passenger side window for a moment then turned toward her father and said, "This will be our little secret dad. I already know exactly what I am going to do, and it will make you and I both proud to be Hildeman's."

Her father delicately stroked his big bushy moustache downward between his thumb and forefingers then remarked, "Whatever you say honey. Whatever ever makes things right for you?"

CHAPTER 19

Training camp went by quickly, and it was now time for Hugo Brody to bring the city of San Diego their sixth Super Bowl title, thus, fulfilling the promise he had made to the entire Charger Nation just five and a half years prior. Monica's wounds had healed physically, but internally she esoterically yearned for her abuser's rightful punishment. Her premeditated revenge crusade had one purpose; to destroy Hugo mentally, physically, spiritually and emotionally. She had devised the perfect vindictive arrangement, and the first game of the new season marked the period as to which the wheels of her plan were put into motion.

Monica not only had reconstructive surgery on her nose to correct the damage, but she also had various cosmetic surgeons make a few additional alterations to her appearance. She had the deep scar on her forehead removed by repeating painful laser treatments every two days. She had painful chemical peels to help improve her skin's quality as well as speed up the recovery process. She also had oral surgery to add porcelain veneers to what little remained of the front row of her teeth. She looked miraculous. However, she was still concerned that she didn't look marvelous enough for Hugo to take the bait.

The outcome of the Charger's first game was just the same as the majority of the others while Hugo 'El Milagro" was at the helm. They won by a large margin, and once again, despite all of his off the field troubles, Hugo was as sharp as ever. He threw the ball magnificently, and completed an incredibly efficient twenty-eight out of thirty passes. After the game, the new and improved Monica waited for the quarterback outside of his locker room. She *somehow* obtained a media pass, and would later go into great detail of how she no longer considered her body as sacred as it once was after being violated. Hugo rushed through the doors and as usual, was accompanied by SWAT, Big Cane and Marinky. The MOF managed to gain his attention by cutting him off, and then stopping him for a photograph. She held her camera up and oddly cocked it like a lever-action rifle. When the photo snapped, she pretended to jerk from the recoil. Hugo struck his signature pose and off he went filtering through the cheering masses once again. He was unperceptive to the strange photographer's "shot," and to the crowd of people, but he moved intently through the strobe of the flashing lights. Suddenly, he stopped like he had been blocked by an invisible wall. He grew pale and looked as if someone punched him in his stomach, taking the wind out of him. He turned back around and made eye contact with what appeared to be a familiar apparition. It was Monica, AND HE REMEMBERED! Even though her appearance had slightly changed, he stared into her as if his eyes were magnetized to some rippling holographic picture. Frightened by the wavering reconstructed image, the young quarterback bolted for his limousine with the crew still clinging to him. Hugo, Big Cane and Marinky all quickly slid into the back of the elongated automobile. At that same time, SWAT promptly raced in the direction of his customary driver's seat. But just as he reached to tug on the handle, the car's engine started and it aggressively drove off. SWAT was left stunned. He had been handling all of the chauffeur duties for quite some time and it was routine for valet to just step out upon his arrival. He couldn't believe that a bodyguard of his caliber could have possibly made such an oversight. SWAT wondered to himself who the man was and how he got into the car. Meanwhile, Hugo, Big Cane and Marinky had no clue what had happened. SWAT immediately attempted to send text messages and call his crew to inform them of the situation, but they usually had the music blaring in the rear of the car, especially after a win. They heard nothing. Even though Hugo was not celebrating, it was not possible for him to hear or react to his cell phone for he was deadened by the seamless vision of his avenger. The limousine veered to the side of the road and halted. The new chauffer opened the back door and summoned for Marinky and Big Cane to step out of the vehicle. They were completely taken by surprise, and looked to be in disbelief. The driver was masked, spoke ruthlessly, and held a medium sized handgun in his right arm. The masked man proceeded to disarm both members of the crew with very little contest. The driver jumped back into the vehicle leaving the remains of Hugo's protection standing in the middle of the road, as well as leaving the vulnerable quarterback to defend himself in solitude.

For the duration of the ride, Hugo furiously pounded his palms on the glass that separated the driver from the passengers. He demanded and screamed out for an explanation for what was happening, but the masked driver ignored futile attempts. Deep down Hugo knew what was occurring. He was well aware that this could be his last limousine ride. He recognized the woman's face from whom he had tortured, and it sparked a recollection that he had wished to suppress forever.

When the cabalistic chauffeur arrived at his destination, two more masked men, who were also built like offensive linemen forced Hugo outside of the car. One man overpowered him to the ground, while the other bashed the backside of his head with the butt end of a larger pistol. The blow had dazed the great quarterback. Within seconds his hands and feet were bound with bulky plastic zip ties; he was gagged and then hauled into an unfurnished chateau that looked to be in the process of being remodeled.

The quarterback was tossed recklessly onto a small bed in one of the far corners of the seemingly vacant house, and was strapped down to the bedposts laying face up by the two giants. His appendages were pulled to the verge of dislocation and his backside hovered about an inch from the mattress. There were two fluorescent upright lights shining down on him, and he had no way of shading his eyes to see out beyond the brightness.

He caught a short glimpse of the two large men exiting the room just before the blinding bulbs shut off. Hugo laid in the darkness wondering what his fate may be. The only sound he could hear was his own rapid breathing, which intensified due to the sheer silence. Hugo was strong, but he knew that he would waste an excruciating amount of energy trying move his arms or legs for they were securely fastened with heavy duty ratchet strap anchors. The silent placidity was beginning to drive Hugo mad. Haphazard thoughts involving torture, death, escaping, Monica Resser, and the fate of his crew cycled repeatedly through his head. He thought of the old Edgar Allan Poe story, *The Pit and Pendulum* that he had read in high school, and anticipated the merciless steel blade tearing into his chest at any moment. He began to feel things crawling all over his skin similar to the punished man from the tale. For a moment he was glad to have his mouth stuffed and gagged for fear that something may meander into it. He couldn't tell if they were cockroaches, spiders or just something that had spawned from his own fretful imagination. Horrific visions of terror dictated all of his thoughts.

Hugo started to hear footsteps circling around the bed. He felt his pants slice up his leg quickly approaching his genitalia. His nostrils pinched together with the sudden burst of inhaled air, startling him to the point where he nearly sucked the gag further down his trachea. The instrument felt like a razor knife but he was not certain. The nocturnal tailor's footsteps echoed throughout the abandoned chateau as Hugo felt a similar slice up his other pant leg. His shirt was also cut following the seams and all of his clothing was then stripped from his suspended body. His absolute immobility left him utterly defenseless, and he started to panic. Just then the intense beams of light kicked on and Monica Resser loomed over her abuser's trembling naked body. Hugo saw her, but was glad to hear the loud humming of the lights. She bent down close to his face and stared into his eyes with utmost hatred. She took a swing at his cheek with an open right hand. Hugo's face grimaced as his head flinched in anticipation of the contact, but the slap never connected.

Monica whispered as the backside of her fingers tickled gently across her target's cheek, "We wouldn't want to hurt that gorgeous face now would we?" She continued with her thumb and index finger squeezing Hugo's nostrils together pinching off all oxygen in-take. Monica laughed diabolically as her enemy squirmed and writhed for one breath of air. "It would be *that* easy," Monica whispered into Hugo's face just before letting loose her grip on his nose. She reached to the floor and pulled out a new cordless electric carving knife. She tested the blade to see if it was charged by pressing the trigger. The high tech motor generated a resonating drone, but more importantly propelled the large blade into a rapid back and forth sawing motion. She inched closer, the trigger fully pressed, toward his male reproductive organ. She just barely nicked it near the base with the rapidly oscillating blade, and quickly jerked away. Then she said, "Let's just end this whole football thing right now," as she drew closer to his right bicep. Monica had a sinister smile on her face. She pushed the churning blade against the skin and notched the flesh of her abuser's golden arm. Hugo's eyes had been closed so tight that his tears of agony squirted from the outer corners, rather than just dribbling down the cheek. He was close to passing out at this point. She moved down slowly near the bottom of the bed and held the dull end of the rotating blade tightly to his toes, pretending to lop them off. She was clearly toying with the object of her rage, and was savoring every second. Monica shut her cordless knife off, and ordered that the lights get turned off as well. In a flash, the room was silent and still once again.

Hugo must have had a panic attack and was out cold, but was awakened to extreme perspiration and once again the gaudy wattage of the fluorescent lights. It was not the MOF who entered the room this second time. It was in fact a man dressed in scrubs and an antibacterial surgical mask. He snapped his rubber gloves on creating a small white puffy cloud that surrounded him. He moved his cold metal table of surgical instruments near the edge of the bed. The strange looking doctor pushed firmly against the side of Hugo's neck, and worked his way down to the top of his throwing shoulder. He slowly walked his fingers from the top portion of the shoulder to a horizontal line seemingly following his clavicle bone. The quarterback's eyelids were so peeled back that the doctor could see all of the veins leading to the iris. The man wearing the sterile gear was expressionless as he rested his fingers on a particularly sensitive area just below the slender right clavicle. He grabbed a scalpel with his free hand and instantly created a tiny incision in between the muscle tissue and the skin's epidermal layer. Just below the bone, the doctor inserted a miniature metallic object, and dabbed the blood with a dry white swatch. After a few stitches, the surgery was complete. The doctor yanked off his gloves and vacated the room, passing

Monica along the way. Hugo was more perplexed than in pain. He wanted to know what had just happened. He honestly thought that he was having another type of nightmare. He glanced over to the woman that he had brutally raped as she casually strolled over to him. Monica snatched the gag from his mouth making a foul face. She aggressively threw the saliva soaked socks down to the floor and they splattered. "Now you listen to me and you listen good. First of all, I have enough evidence to get you locked up for a very long time. Secondly, I could've easily taken your life tonight see (and would have liked to) but I am not a deranged and demented deviant like yourself." Hugo just laid there like a cadaver. "Thirdly, my good friend inserted a small tracking device just below your right shoulder bone to ensure that you will not attempt to do anything irrational. In fact, he could have placed the device anywhere, but I intentionally ordered him to place it in that specific location for it will cause severe discomfort when your skin and muscle tissue begin to reject the foreign object. From this point on, you will no longer be Hugo "The Miracle" Brody. You will be Monica's new obedient boyfriend. If you try to remove the accessory, or visit someplace that is off-limits, I will turn you over to the police and you Mr. Brody will spend the rest of your worthless life in prison. Everything that you have done to me has been carefully documented, complete with photos taken soon after the rape, and attached to the case files. There is plenty of proof that you once raped me and had attempted to kill me not that long ago. So call it blackmail, call it a threat, call it retribution, or you can just embrace it as an opportunity to live outside of imprisonment, but we are going to have to work out an agreement before I let you walk out of here."

Hugo peered at his nemesis in hostility, yet with a sense of understanding. He asked, "You mean you will let me live? You're saying that you will allow me to walk out of here tonight?"

Monica shook her head in agreement and replied, "Yes, but only under certain conditions." Hugo helplessly tied and tormented for hours was just basically looking for a way out. He knew he could conjure up a way out of this mess sooner or later. She said, "I am now *YOUR GIRL*. We will put on a little show for the public, and you must act as if you are madly in love with me." Hugo awkwardly agreed to the first stipulation. Monica continued, "If at any point you should tell someone of our little secret, remove the tracking chip, or if anyone finds out because you've tipped them off, I go straight to the police."

Hugo was clearly following, but he interjected, "Okay, fine but why not just kill me and get it over with?"

Monica, obviously irritated, responded fiercely, "I want back some of what you've taken from me. I want to experience the fame and the glory. I want to be adored and idolized by all of the insignificant people of the world." She added, "If at any point I feel that you are unfaithful to me, or I have tracked your movement to another female's address, then I will have you killed in the most agonizingly way imaginable." After she was convinced that her new pet would play along with her little game, Monica released him. She had her hired help drop the naked quarterback off just a few miles from the hotel in which he was staying just before daybreak. His trek to his hotel strangely duplicated Monica's unclothed walk of survival to the service station with wings. He hid his vulnerable body behind trees from passing vehicles; he battled the blistering pain that surged from his tender feet, and vindictive thoughts passed in and out of his head throughout his embarrassing plight. Monica's premeditated plot had been launched flawlessly. There was no better form of entertainment than the delight she felt while following her enemy's every pace on the handheld tracking transmitter.

CHAPTER 20

"How could you let this happen," Hugo repeated numerous times to SWAT, Big Cane and Marinky. The quarterback was on the verge of firing his crew of inept bodyguards after his abduction, but after several apologies, Hugo decided that he may need them now more than ever. He described and explained the torment and torture that he had suffered through the previous night, but he carefully reworked the recount just enough to leave out everything involving the psychopath Monica Resser, as well as the instillation of the tracking device. He showed his commitment to the agreement that Monica had entrusted him with by not telling anyone about their union. Hugo knew that his other choice was to serve a long term sentence in jail.

Hugo attended practice the next day, but he did not participate. He conjured up the standard story that most professional athletes use when they need a day of rest; the dreaded groin pull. The truth was that his whole body ached. His joints on his appendages were terribly sore from being pulled and stretched; he had gauze pads adhered to both feet for the absorption of various fluids, and even the small slit were his tiny tracking device had been inserted felt unpleasant.

Monica had certainly achieved her initial goal. Hugo was experiencing physical discomfort, despite showing really no signs of any visible injuries, and immense mental anguish. She picked him up from practice, drove him everywhere, and knew exactly where to find her man at all times. It was bizarre how not even one member of the crew thought it was peculiar how Hugo's first real girlfriend in quite a few years seemed to only cling to him when in public. In fact, she had only been to The Donjon one other time to "pretend" sleep with Hugo, and to discuss her part in the relationship with SWAT and the boys. She was doing a fantastic job so far as his new faux girlfriend, but Hugo was struggling in that department. When the clever Monica Resser had confessed her genuine love for Hugo to SWAT and the rest of the bodyguards, they collectively agreed that it was definitely about time that their boss finally got himself a steady girl to help settle him down. The burly bodyguards also remembered Monica from the MOF party, and they had a hunch that the two were crazy for each other from that night on. After all, they knew nothing about Hugo's disgusting secret sex crime. Once again, the three behemoths played a prominent role in swaying Hugo's inner psyche, despite not knowing all of the facts. As Hugo made a conscientious decision to remain secretive about his predicament, all three of the bodyguards congratulated the couple on their newfound love. To the surprise of Hugo, they all approved of her and saw her as just what he needed after everything he had been through. He undoubtedly thought that letting her into his life so suddenly would raise some red flags with his protectors. But then again, these are the same imbeciles who were unable to stop a simple kidnapping.

Hugo Brody, for the first time in his entire football career, took three consecutive days off from practicing because he was truly in a significant amount of pain. He looked very poor throwing the football in the two practices in which he did take part, leading up to the game on Sunday. His coach had no choice but to let him start the game, the team's owner and the Charger Nation would've gone mad over a performance based benching. However, it was clear from his performance that something was definitely wrong. Hugo and his Chargers lost 34-7. The obviously afflicted quarterback threw four interceptions and had none of the usual zip on his throws. He also was described as being "disoriented" by his teammates who joined him in the huddle before each play.

After the game, Hugo was consistently asked, by his head coach as well as members of the media, if he was injured. They also inquired about the attractive female that had been seen just about everywhere with him. Monica was actually even seated next to him as the press fired question after question. She just sat there smiling, as her false lover stumbled uncomfortably on each question. They were often seen dining together, or posing for photographs with each other, and the paparazzi loved it. Pictures of the wicked pair landed on loads of smut magazine covers that littered the shelves of stores all over the globe. Hugo tirelessly denied any injury and repeatedly told the media that Monica was his true love. He resumed practicing daily to try to make up for his embarrassing defeat, but after several weeks, Hugo Brody could not be anymore vanquished. The Chargers had lost their next four consecutive games, and were now a woeful 1-5 to start the season. It looked like the twenty-seven year-old star quarterback had lost his grip on life, and his game. He was falling apart.

The primary focus of the maniacal media once again blamed his downfall on his new girlfriend. They gave up on the notion that he may be playing with some secretive injury. And the idea of him just simply losing his passion for the game was quickly overlooked. His new relationship was far more incredibly juicy, so all forms of entertainment opted for the bad luck charm story. Everyone seemed to be calling for Monica's head. Monica's plan up to this point had worked to perfection; however she did not anticipate all of the threats coming her way.

Monica was omnipresent as she continuously reminded her fabricated flame of the details of their agreement, as well as the consequences. However, death did not frighten her pawn and even the thought of spending the rest of his life in prison no longer intimidated Hugo Brody anymore. He was sick of it all, and had clearly reached his threshold. He determined that he was finished with this coercive allegiance. He simply could not take anymore losing, and was on the brink of being benched. He could no longer stand being controlled by some evil manipulative woman, while at the same time pretending to be her lover. He started to catalogue his options; he was either going to do a better job of killing her this time, just break down and tell the police everything and accept the consequences, or he was going to get the dross tracking implant removed and disappear into obscurity. He realized that if this were any other MOF or ex-girlfriend, Hugo knew that he could've just forked over some exorbitant lump sum of money for her to keep her mouth shut. But, he was well aware from the beginning that Monica was much more interested in the glitz and glam, rather than wealth.

A few hours before the power couple was scheduled to take part in a commercial for shampoo that would ironically forever link the pair to cleanliness, Hugo snatched a sharp knife from the kitchen drawer. He carefully folded his shirt around the knife to conceal it as he restlessly passed his crew to go up the stairs. He stood in front of the master bathroom suite mirror and held the knifepoint against his skin near where the scarring had formed over the implanted device. He took a deep breath and was close to inserting the knife to carve out the persistent tracking gadget when the gruesome thought of operating on his own body made him queasy. He became very weak, and could not go through with. Instead, he thought of a plan to eliminate Monica Resser all together. His reflective smile in the mirror at the preconceived notion reinforced his own approval. In a sense he would be free even if the police *were* to find out. His scheme was simple. He would wait until after tomorrow night's home game with the Baltimore Ravens, which he truly hoped to play in. Then, after Monica arrived to pick him up and the pair had saturated in the flashbulbs for awhile, on the way home he would requisition her for a quick stop at a nearby service station for something to quench his thirst. He would tell SWAT and his gang of worthless protectors, who always followed closely behind in a SUV, to go ahead home and that he was just stopping for a drink. He was well aware that all stops were prohibited, so he would have to act desperately dehydrated. Then, his plan was to strangle her to death before she could put the gearshift in drive. He decided that he would just drop her dead body off somewhere along the highway. He wanted no blood, so even though he knew it would be a struggle, he decided that it was his cleanest option. After plotting and deliberating his new deranged plan, instead of smiling in front of the mirror he caught a glimpse of his former self and became completely unexpressive. He thought about his father Sebastian, and what he would think of his son. Hugo mouthed to his reflection, "What happened to you?" He was extremely nervous about going through with it.

CHAPTER 21

Hugo doubted whether or not he could actually kill another human being by choking them with his own bare hands, and the hours leading up to the game were tense and fretful. He brooded heavily but always tried to reassure himself that it was indeed the only possible option. It was even more distressing when Monica arrived to pick him up two hours early. Now, whether Monica Resser had somehow sensed his turning in character, or she was tipped off by a member of the always lingering crew, it may never be known. But just a few minutes before departing for a home game versus the Baltimore Ravens, the deceptive female grabbed a sports drink from the refrigerator, unscrewed the lid and added six drops from a dropper of clear liquid into the bottle. She tightened the lid to make it look like it was never opened and shook the contents viciously. She then proceeded to remove the three other plastic bottles of thirst quencher leaving only one to choose from. After Hugo was finished getting ready, he did indeed customarily grab the last sports drink from the kitchen on his way out the door, not knowing it had been laced with a sedative.

Monica and the crew were waiting for the star quarterback in their vehicles and Hugo was the last one out of The Donjon. Monica peered out over top of the steering wheel attentively at the polluted bottle in Hugo's hand. As Hugo approached Monica's outdated tiny sedan, the thought of attempting to pay her off once again crossed his mind. It intrigued him mostly because she drove an old dilapidated car, and she didn't really wear expensive clothing. It appeared as though she was not wealthy, so why hasn't she attempted to extort him for millions? For the entire ride to the stadium, Hugo envisioned and contemplated his plan. The cursed strangling invaded and clouded all other thoughts. He continued to restore confidence in himself that he could carry out this horrible deed if it truly was his only option. But, perhaps there could be a monetary amount that could make Monica Resser disappear forever.

When the vile duo reached the stadium, Monica had taken her usual seat in the front row on the fifty yard line, and Hugo took part in various warm-up exercises. Monica observed carefully from the stands as her phony lover finished imbibing her concoction during warm-ups. Hugo Brody did get the starting nod on this night basically, as his coach had informed him, because the team really did not have a quality backup quarterback, and the owners have far too much invested in him. Hugo looked sharp in all of his pre-game warm-up tosses, but on the first snap from scrimmage even the casual fan could tell something wasn't right. The powerful effects of some type of drug began to slowly take hold as he stumbled while trying to complete a simple hand-off to the running back. When he returned to the huddle, one of his lineman asked in a slow southern drawl, "Are you gonna' be alright dude?"

Hugo, looking about half coherent, responded arrogantly, "My spike got caught, I'll be fine." He received the next play via hand signal from his coach, but the toxins had taken over his memory so he just called out the name of the first play that he could remember. The play he announced was a pass. Hugo wobbled up under center for the second play of the game. He leaned rearward a little further than usual as he squatted, and he started to bark out his signature cadence. His own players would later testify that the voice they heard that day didn't even resemble their proud quarterback's. They feared something had gone wrong. Unfortunately, the center snapped the ball as soon as he thought he had heard the word "go" just as he had been trained to do ever since he played in his first pee-wee league game. Hugo was actually looking up toward the sky when the football made contact with his hands. As the ball struck his palms, Hugo jerked backwards clumsily two or three paces and then collapsed. He buckled as if someone from the stands had shot him in the spine just as his haunting reoccurring dream had predicted. His facemask dug deeply into the grassy surface leaving behind a short, but deep divot. The paid attendance expelled a collective gasp as thousands of hands propelled in an upward motion covering their mouths in unison. The medical staff rushed on to the field in an ambulance with the two rear doors swinging open as they approached Hugo's motionless body. Members of the medical staff ran close behind to catch the stretcher as it exploded from the double doors. They left his helmet on as they turned him over on his back to check for signs of breathing. An abundance of grass and sod had accumulated between the bars of his facemask creating a dense shield. Four men hoisted the quarterback atop the stretcher and quickly strapped him in. Only a devastating event of this magnitude could bring such an eerie silence to an overflowing stadium of obsessed football fans. He was carted into the rear of the medically equipped vehicle and the driver swiftly sped away.

Monica, with tears streaming down both cheeks and her body falsely trembling, shot up from the reserved front row seat. She raced up to the luxury box where SWAT and the others were already in motion heading toward the elevators. All four of them fled in SWAT's SUV to the nearest hospital in shock and disbelief. The game resumed after the lengthy delay with an unsettling atmosphere similar to being at a wake.

CHAPTER 22

When the concerned party arrived at the hospital, Hugo was isolated in a room and they were informed that he had been breathing the entire time. He had an oxygen mask covering his nose and mouth and an IV inserted into his forearm. His eyes were still closed, but it was clear that his chest was moving up and down.

Dr. Dunn first briefed the affected individuals, but was careful not to disclose too much information. He said that on the surface this looks like an overdose and that they will be running tests and monitoring his status until he awakens. He also inquired about his patient's immediate family, to which SWAT responded, "He has none. We are his immediate family." Then Dr. Dunn tersely informed the members of the media that had assembled in the hospital's press room on Hugo's current status. In such a short time, amazingly there were at least one hundred members of the press anxiously awaiting any information on the twenty-seven year old superstar. The video of the collapse was being replayed and discussed on every tiny television that the hospital had hanging. When Dr. Dunn mentioned that Hugo's fall was not caused by extreme fatigue or dehydration the media mob did not even seem shocked at all. Based on the celebrity quarterback's befouled reputation, most people in general presumed that Hugo's plunge was probably drug related. No one in that press room was surprised to hear the doctor reveal that this event could have been due to a possible drug overdose, but nonetheless the room quickly became more energetic. A dozen reporters shouted out questions all at the same time, papers were being thrashed about, and the amount of chatter had increased significantly. The story a possible overdose, in combination with the caliber of celebrity involved, had the entertainment insiders drooling over the excitement. They couldn't dream up a more exhilarating story.

Monica's feign tears had fooled the doctor, but the next man in uniform would be a little more difficult. One lone police officer, Officer William Worthy, entered Hugo's room quietly and asked to speak with Ms. Resser alone. SWAT was the only other visitor in the room at that time, and he gladly granted the policeman's request. The bodyguard ducked out of the room to join Big Cane and Marinky in the waiting area where the men watched highlights of their boss's disaster repeatedly on television. Officer Worthy was a younger cop that looked to be around thirty years old. His hair was cut and styled abnormally edgy for a police officer. He looked at Monica's pseudo-sad face with his ultra blue eyes and said, "I just need to ask you a few questions. I know you've been through a lot here tonight, but the doctor out there told me that Mr. Brody is going to be just fine. There is nothing to worry about okay." The confident young cop seemed as if he had practiced, rehearsed and repeated that same introduction about a thousand times already in his brief career. Monica gave the officer a faint nod as she continued to catch tears in a tissue. Officer Worthy went on, "Let's start with the basic information first. Miss, what is your name and address?"

Monica looked extremely nervous after the officer only inquired about her name. Her legs moved further underneath her chair and the young policeman took notice. "My name is Monica sir, and I live at 266 Estate Drive, Covelo, California 95428."

Worthy wrote down the information in a tiny spiraled notebook then proceeded to say, "Monica what? What is your *last* name?" Once again Monica shuffled her legs and gave a shy look of embarrassment. She replied nervously, "Resser, sir."

The cop observed her unmistaken anxiety and promptly went on with the questioning. He said, "Who else was present at Hugo's house when you picked him up?" She gave the policeman the nicknames of the members of Hugo's security team, and explained that she had never learned their real names. Officer Worthy said, "That's okay, I have to ask them some questions too so I'll get their full names later. Don't worry about it." Oddly, as the questions started to become more intrusive, Monica seemed to grow more comfortable. She stopped fidgeting so much; basically because she knew that he was a keen observer who had been analyzing her nonverbal communication. After the officer had inquired about the length of time she had spent with Hugo before leaving for the game, she noticeably became quite talkative, almost flirty. She was clearly trying to distract him. Finally he asked, "Did you see Hugo take any medication before you all departed? Or, did you see him drinking anything at all?"

Monica playfully flicked some of her brown hair away from her face and replied, "I didn't see him take anything, but he was in the bathroom right before we left for an awful long time. And he carried a sports drink out of the house with him to the game. But he always has one of those before practices or games."

The officer jotted down the necessary details and said, "Okay, one last question. Have you seen anyone strange hanging around Mr. Brody over the passed few days?"

Monica shook her head and responded, "No, I haven't seen anyone unusual around Hugo, but if I remember someone I will definitely contact you Mr. Officer." Officer Worthy finished scribbling in the pocket-sized notebook and stood up from his chair. He had spotted Monica's curious mood changing behavior, as well as her apprehensiveness. He remained very professional, and was neither enticed nor amused by her mischievous attempts to distract him.

Before escorting the young female out the door, he looked closely into her eyes and whispered firmly, "If any of the information that you have given me turns out to be false, you will be called into the station for further investigation as the lead suspect. Obstruction of justice is a serious offense." Monica bitterly turned and walked out of the room. He ordered for her to send SWAT in next.

SWAT spent about the same amount of time in the room with Officer Worthy as Monica, as did Big Cane and Marinky when their time came. Monica paced back and forth on various hospital floors wondering if the officer ended his brief interrogations with the members of the crew in the same manner. She returned to the waiting area and sat next to SWAT and Big Cane and pretended to watch television for awhile. She interrupted the men's concentration and asked, "Did Officer Worthy accuse either of you of lying after he was done with all of the questions?" The behemoths looked at each other dumbfounded, and then glanced back toward Monica. Both men said in agreement, "No." Then they continued to devote their full attention once again to the television program. Just then the door opened on Hugo's room. Marinky walked over after his round of questioning and sat on the other side of SWAT. All three of the men seemed virtually unaffected by the tiny probing session, but Monica's face showed signs of distress. Officer Worthy strolled over to where all four were sitting and said, "I'd like to thank you all for your time. If you should think of anything else, or hear anything new please give me a ring." He handed each person a card to contact him and walked to the elevator. While waiting for the elevator, he shot one more glance across the waiting room with his two icy blues and noticed that Monica was already reentering Hugo's room while the others continued to sit comfortably. The young officer seemed to have his doubts about her, like many he was skeptical of their sudden relationship. He suspected that that beautiful girl played some role in the calamitous collapse on the football field earlier that day.

CHAPTER 23

As soon as Officer William Worthy returned to the police
station he verified all of the correct background information on
the three bodyguards, as well as the address for The Donjon.
He saved Monica Resser for last because he considered her his
prime suspect. Even though a lacing case and possible perjury
would be considered lesser offenses, he pursued the case with
utmost diligence simply because it was so high profile. At most
the guilty person responsible would only serve a year in prison.
The competent policeman searched and located a residence at the
address Monica had relayed to him. However, his data reported
that there was no one by the name Monica Resser currently
residing there. In fact, that particular dwelling housed a totally
different family all together. He thought to himself that he had
encountered this problem a few times in the past and even though
it could be a false address, the system sometimes is unaware of

the most current changes. Or, it is possible that she could be one of those freeloader, not poor but homeless, types. After searching throughout his entire police database, Officer Worthy quickly realized that this case was much more complicated. There were no records of a Monica Resser in the entire state of California. He also found no record at all in the national database of a person existing under the name Monica Resser.

After discovering that he had been provided with a phony name and address, the young officer determined that he at least had enough to haul the young lady into the station for further questioning. He told his captain what he had found out about the girl, and once again, even though spiking one's drink and providing false information were minor violations, Worthy's boss still warned him about a case of this caliber. After about a ten minute precautionary deliberation where Officer Worthy heard the words "never underestimate" repeatedly, his captain decided to assign him a partner that he was not particularly fond of to begin with. Both men left the station with one objective, to bring in the young woman who refers to herself as Monica Resser for further questioning.

Officer Worthy, since it was his squad car, decided that he would drive his new partner to the hospital where Hugo was receiving care. The young officer drove fast, but not impatiently as he assumed Hugo would be staying at the hospital overnight with the woman by his side. Officer Worthy updated his slightly overweight partner about the specifics of the case as they walked through the waiting area. Only SWAT remained sitting in the same uncomfortable hospital chair that looked much too small for his enormous body.   The two policemen approached the bodyguard and asked him if Hugo had awakened yet. SWAT replied, "No, I don't think so."

Worthy then asked, "Hey where did everyone else go?"

SWAT looked like he had fallen asleep at some point between Worthy's two visits.   He seemed a bit addled and his black curly hair was flattened down on one side. The massive bodyguard said, "Big Cane and Marinky left right after ya'll interviewed us. They had some double date thing planned and I told them that I'd call or text as soon as Hugo wakes up." Monica has been in and out of that room all night long, so she's probably still in there." The young officer thanked the big guy, and started toward Hugo's room.   Even though he visualized the prime suspect sitting there at the foot of her lover's bed weeping, he had a bad feeling in his gut telling him that the great quarterback may be dead in his bed or that something terrible awaited him behind the closed door. He had feared upon entry that his primary suspect had gone. The two men approached the door which they had anticipated being closed because it was far beyond visitor's hours. The room was dark with only the tiny television providing a ray of light. Officer Worthy turned the door handle and pushed the heavy wooden hospital door open swiftly, hoping to catch his main suspect off guard.   Instead, it was both police officers who were not prepared for what was behind the door. There was no sign of the woman as Officer William Worthy gingerly peeled back the curtain that safeguarded Hugo's bed from any visitors. Worthy's face grew extremely pale as he staggered clumsily to get a closer look at what was under the covers. The form resembled a large body, but when Worthy and his partner pulled back the bedding they saw shoulder pads, pillows and clothes strategically placed to make one believe that the bed was still occupied. The IV had been removed from Hugo's arm and remained dangling a few inches from the shoulder pads resting on the bed sheet. Both men where stunned. Officer Worthy noticed that the window had been opened so he quickly ran over to scan the area. He knew that they had not been gone for long because heat could still be felt omitting from Hugo's turned off monitor, and the bedding also remained warm to the touch. However, Hugo's room was on the sixth floor of the hospital, and even though there was a roof just a few feet below, the officers wondered how a woman could possibly get a 220 pound man out of a window and off of a roof by herself. He figured either she had help or they slid by hospital staff undetected to the nearby elevator or steps. Worthy ran outside the room and glanced down the nearest flight of stairs, but saw or heard no one. Both officers glanced at the bedside chart to see what time it was when the last nurse completed her rounds. Nurse Cassie had initialed her name in the box just ten minutes prior to their arrival. They were even more baffled. Officer Worthy directed his large partner to find this nurse "Cassie" and ask her what she had seen in Hugo's room. He also told his new partner to make sure he asks her exactly what duties she had performed as well. Officer Worthy basically sprinted toward SWAT, who remained snug in his seat. He said, "You're supposed to be this man's bodyguard! I would've fired you a long time ago. Did you see anything?"

SWAT stared intensely at the policeman and stood up from

his chair angrily. It was almost as if the huge bodyguard was going to try to intimidate the smaller Officer Worthy.

Worthy exclaimed, "Sit down, big boy! You mean to tell me that you saw NOTHING!"

SWAT really didn't know what to make of the situation. He returned to his seat and simply said, "What happened?"

Officer Worthy, obviously disgusted at this point, waved his hand in the air and said, "Your pal Hugo is gone. The woman you all know as Monica is gone too. And let me guess, the almighty protector slept through it all."

SWAT was feeling extraordinarily uncomfortable; he couldn't believe the nerve of this creep. If he wasn't wearing a badge, he probably would've died in that waiting room. SWAT admitted that he had fallen asleep for awhile, and that whatever happened may have occurred during that time. He said, "I didn't really feel like my man's life was in danger when he was layin' in a hospital bed." Officer Worthy saw his partner walking toward him so he stopped his tirade and listened to what Nurse Cassie had to say. His partner took out his notes and read word for word the information he had obtained from the nurse which even further irritated the impatient officer. He said that the only duties Cassie performed was that she just initially signed her name in, and she checked the patient's bedpan to see if it needed emptied which it did not. The officer also pointed out the fact that Nurse Cassie was "smokin' hot". She didn't bother to check to see if he was breathing, or if he was even indeed still in his bed. She also said that she remembered that the girl was not in the room with the patient at that time, and if the window was open, she didn't notice.

Officer Worthy had to check with all of the medical staff present on that particular floor just to make sure none of the employees had seen anything, but it was just as useless as Cassie. He was completely bewildered by the fact that not one nurse, doctor, or janitor had seen a woman struggling to smuggle a patient out of their hospital.

The young officer sat and deliberated his next move. He questioned how a woman, albeit physically fit based on her appearance, could carry out a man who weighed about one-hundred pounds more than her, and who had been out cold. A thought that perhaps SWAT wasn't sleeping, and possibly he aided in the escape had occurred to him, but he let it subside for the moment. He already had too much to take on. He contacted the crime lab and the local law enforcement from nearby towns to sweep the entire place. He wanted to find out if they were completely off of hospital grounds, how the two had escaped, where they had escaped from, and if any surveillance cameras were able to capture anything. Then he would contact missing persons to try to notify them that the incredibly popular quarterback, Hugo Brody, may have possibly been abducted.

Officer Worthy, grabbed a cup of coffee from the vending machine on the sixth floor and rested his head on his hand braced against the top of the machine. He thought to himself, no name, no address, no license plate number, and an incapacitated victim kidnapped from a hospital; he wondered what he had gotten himself into.

CHAPTER 24

The search and sweep completed by several local police departments, as well as their mobile crime labs did clarify some details. The suspect, referred to as Monica, did in fact drive away with Hugo as a security camera located in the parking garage revealed footage of the woman hauling his motionless body backwards on a recliner with wheels. She struggled to pull his limp body into the backseat of her red sedan. Hugo was only wearing a hospital gown, and had no shoes on, yet the woman left the heels of his feet drag on the jagged concrete surface. Tests later determined from blood samples taken off of the concrete did match Hugo's blood type which luckily, the hospital had on file. The pair was no longer near the facility, and according to the recorded time of departure they had left twenty minutes before Officer Worthy and his partner had arrived. Another camera stationed at the parking garage's exit captured the most vital piece of evidence in the entire search. The camera was able to provide authorities with a license plate number with which they could possibly identify the young female.

It was not clear how she managed to get her supposed boyfriend out of the hospital undetected, however after exploring the possibility of a dramatic rooftop escape, there were no clear signs that they had chosen that particular method. The men leading the investigation assumed that since the stairs and the elevator were so close in proximity, that the pair most likely had taken that route. Officer Worthy started to realize after the window and roof theory was debunked, that they weren't dealing with the average criminal. He knew that this young lady was cunning, intelligent and capable of creating new options just to intentionally complicate the investigation. Another notable piece of evidence gathered by the cameras was SWAT getting up from his chair in the waiting area, and bringing back a lounging recliner with wheels, perhaps from a nurse's station or doctor's desk.

The most peculiar morsel of evidence gathered at the hospital was accumulated by the mobile crime lab division. Tests had been run on the hospital bed linens which detected heavy traces of vaginal secretions. It was presumed that the young female had engaged in sexual intercourse with the star quarterback most likely while he was incapacitated, but lab employees found it bizarre that no male reproductive fluids were found on the sheets. Other possible scenarios had to be explored, but it appeared as if she raped him before she abducted him. Thus, adding an element to the investigation that gave it whole new serious, yet sinister twist.

The call to notify missing persons must have tipped off the Federal Bureau of Investigation. Officer Worthy was informed that the FBI will allow him to continue the investigation, but only under the wings of the Bureau, and more specifically without a partner. William Worthy was relieved. He was much more comfortable working on his own.

The search for Hugo Brody intensified with the possibility of a sexual assault on top of his abduction, and the license plate number gave investigators a bona fide lead. There were several detectives within the Bureau working the case, and the local police officer William Worthy became lost in the shuffle quite often. Every news channel became obsessed with the strange case and the abduction made national, as well international headlines. The bubbly blonde on the entertainment insider obviously had some minor work done in anticipation of an increase in viewers. Her face appeared to rewind in time and her hair was freshly cut and dyed. An older member of the FBI's investigative team who had followed the media coverage extensively up to this point made the comment, "Even if the president was assassinated, you wouldn't see the monsters of media in such chaos."

Members of the Bureau gathered in the hospital lobby to hear an informal debriefing about the identification of the young female suspect. One of the men in charge of the investigation said quietly but with youthful exuberance, "You guys are never gonna believe who our main suspect is. Her true name is Monica Hildeman. She is the daughter of the National Football League's

Mike Hildeman, head coach for the Seattle Seahawks." Most of the agents in the FBI managed to stay abreast on professional football, as did the local cop, so they had all heard of head coach Mike Hildeman before. All of the men and women who had assembled to hear the prime suspect's real name were so proud and so grateful at that very moment for it reassured them that they had certainly chosen the perfect profession. Officer Worthy interjected, but with just a small sliver of the agents' attentiveness, "Hey, didn't the Chargers beat the Seahawks in like the last three or four Super Bowls? There is your motive right there." The agents were shocked to hear something so profound come from the lips of a local officer. "Good thinking, nice work Worthy," exclaimed the man in charge.

At least six agents piled into two separate black SUV's while Officer Worthy drove unaccompanied in his squad car to a small airport outside of San Diego. Upon arrival, the six agents and Officer Worthy scurried up an awaiting ladder aboard a small private jet. The destination was close in proximity to the Hildeman Estate located in central Washington. The agents immediately began to outline a tactical plan once again leaving Officer Worthy pretty much out of the loop. He did happen to overhear the slight buzz over whether or not Monica would be present at the house or not. Even though her father's estate was listed in the FBI database as her primary place of residence, the agents discussed that the Hildeman family was quite an aristocratic bunch. They owned property, possibly a cabin in northern Washington, a beach house near Coos Bay in Oregon, and a recently purchased large mansion in San Marcos, California. As the jet engines fired,

Worthy inquired to an agent sitting closest to him, "Why didn't we search the house closest to the hospital first? It hasn't even been a full day yet since the two have gone missing."

The older agent responded loudly over all of the engine noise, "We have teams of agents traveling to all of the Hildeman's properties. Plus, that one in San Marcos is vacant. From what I hear there aren't even any walls in that place." The jet began to move forward getting ready to take flight. The agent, almost shouting to Officer Worthy said, "Besides, Daddy's little girl is in trouble. Who do you think she'll run to? Oh, Ya' the Hildeman's have a jet too." The policeman nodded in understanding, as the agent sort of smirked at him. As the small jet began to liftoff, the young police officer had a hunch that they would not find Monica Hildeman at her father's house. He based is suspicion on the obvious fact that it had only been approximately twenty hours since she had taken Hugo from the hospital near San Diego. He wished that he was better informed for he would have rather been in his car cruising toward the address in San Marcos with the other team of agents. He felt as if he was wasting valuable time.

CHAPTER 25

The small jet landed on the weathered runway of what looked to be an old deserted airport. The agents informed the young police officer that he would be accompanying them in one of the SUV's for about a forty minute ride to the Hildeman Estate. Once the team had reached its destination, they quickly dispersed into positions surrounding bottom floor windows and all other visible exit points. Two federal agents wearing dark blue performance jackets approached the main entrance of the luxurious property and rang the doorbell. The head coach, Mike Hildeman answered the door and immediately ushered them into the house. All of the other agents, as well as the police officer, were ordered to stay in position until they were given the consent to search inside the premises. The first thing Mike Hildeman said was, "She's not here, you can search if you want to. I have no idea where my daughter is." The coach of the

Seahawks managed to appear quite unaffected externally for a father who has repeatedly seen his daughter's face on television for all of the wrong reasons, but the experienced agents were able to quickly see right through his ignorant facade. He fidgeted slightly with his eyeglasses as he told the agents that he has only heard from Monica twice by phone in the past month. And that the last line of communication was at least two weeks prior to this latest ridiculous episode. He mentioned that once she became Hugo's girl, she basically stopped calling and visiting the house. He also convincingly stated, as he made eye contact for the very first time, that the couple probably had some issue that needs resolved, and he was confident that the two would work it out. Whether or not he was reassuring the police or himself that everything would be fine was the question that many agents were left with. Nevertheless, his behavior was suspicious.

His cooperative hospitable persona shifted quickly as a member of the team shouted, "I found something!" from the upper floor.

Mike raised his voice, "I told you, she hasn't been here in months!" And then he began to oddly stroke his fluffy white moustache.

One of the agents found a large brown envelope in one of Monica's dresser drawers containing what appeared to be photographs of her at a time when she had been badly bruised and scratched. One of the photos focused on a large gash on her upper forehead, and another centered on her tiny sharp triangular teeth. One of the men made a comment referring to her transformation. He said, "Wow, this doesn't even look like our suspect." One of the agents sealed the contents in a large plastic bag and confiscated it for evidence.

The two men questioning Mike Hildeman replaced their inquisitive soft method with an arsenal of investigative questions about the newly acquired evidence. They also fired a shot at the possible motive for the abduction. Mike was certainly uneasy as he incessantly stroked his moustache, but he tried hard to remain calm and quiet for the most part. He said that he knew nothing of the photos, and he blatantly laughed at the notion of his team repeatedly losing to Hugo's Chargers as having anything to do with this mess. He then proceeded to tell the challenging agents that he would not say another word until his lawyer was present.

The police officer and the agents left the estate feeling very confident with what they had achieved. They were positive that the coach knew more than he had confessed. They were also aware that they could take him to the department headquarters at any time based on motive, but were comfortable with leaving him squirm for short time while they located his daughter. Before entering the black SUV's once again to drive back over to the small airport, the federal agent in charge urged everyone in attendance to try to understand exactly how crucial it is that they find Monica Hildeman based on the photographs they had gathered, and the premise that this case could possibly be revenge based. He said that the plan now was to launch an all out search for their suspect, and when they find her, the FBI will haul both father and daughter in for comprehensive interrogation. Teams of agents, and strategic plans were quickly put into effect by the Bureau.

The team of agents that searched the cabin located in northern Washington found nothing, but some of those men were ordered to stay and keep the place under close surveillance. The other unit that had searched the newly purchased mansion was greeted by several construction workers, who just happened to be contracted by Mike Hildeman to renovate the old chateau. The workers on site were questioned but none of the men confessed to ever seeing Monica Hildeman on, or near the grounds.

Older model red sedans were being pulled over on highways in the states along the west coast. There were news broadcasts urging people to contact the crime hotline if they should see Monica Hildeman/Resser or star quarterback Hugo Brody. The Feds were relentlessly pursuing every possible lead. They had stake-outs, wiretaps and men and women patrolling the internet traffic. Police K-9 units were sent to search all of the Hildeman's properties. Police dogs even rummaged through The Donjon and combed the woods surrounding the mysterious mansion. The intelligent Sheppard dogs located a smashed sedan with some of Hugo's blood on the steering wheel hidden behind The Donjon, but that was it. Surveillance was set up at Sebastian's gravesite. Even though some of Hugo's deranged fans held some type of strange nightly vigil near his tomb, no new information surfaced. It seemed as if the two dignitaries had just fallen off the face of the earth.

The search for the pair was expansive, but most of the men and women investigating the case were growing weary of false leads, phony clues, and dead-end tips. Items of interest were turning up everywhere. Hugo's shoulder pads were mysteriously returned to his locker in the San Diego Chargers practice facility. Nobody knew how the pads got there from the hospital, but they were uniquely designed quarterback pads that only Hugo could have afforded to own. A second sweep of The Donjon's grounds, completed by K-9 units, revealed a yet another misdirection. Over in one of the far-off fields, trained police dogs were completely aroused near the base of the old mannequin's post. They sniffed and snorted as if the dummy concealed cooked meat in its pockets. What the skilled dogs detected however, was the scent of squirrel blood. Someone had taken the time to shoot two squirrels, slice the small animals to allow blood flow, and neatly tuck them under the mannequin's Charger jersey. Police and investigators were frustrated to the point of disgust by all of the deliberate distractions.

Nearly six days had passed when Officer William Worthy went back on his original hunch. After checking in with his superiors back at his local department, he drove his police cruiser to the address in San Marcos, California. There he found two federal agents continuously observing from across the street in a white pickup truck trying to simulate additional construction workers. Officer Worthy, approached in street clothes, introduced himself to the men and asked if they had seen anything. The agents looked anything but inconspicuous in their yellow hardhats, perfectly clean jeans and bright orange vests. The men shook hands and the young cop had to stop himself from erupting into laughter when he felt how unexposed and uncalloused the two men's hands were. Both agents seemed delighted just to see someone relevant. The younger of the two said, "We've been out here for six days, and have not seen anyone but these few construction guys." Worthy inquired about the nights, and the younger agent replied, "A different team comes in at night with no vehicle and they haven't seen anyone at all around this place." The police officer asked the agents if it would be okay for him to take a look inside and neither objected.

Officer Worthy, armed with his police issued handgun, pocket notebook and a pen, walked through the front doorway which had neither a door nor hinges attached. He remembered the agent on the jet telling him that there weren't any walls in the house, but there were a few newer walls standing and several old barriers that have yet to be torn down or gutted. The entire place appeared to be in the midst of a complete renovation. The cop approached several of the laborers and introduced himself as Officer Worthy, but most of them seemed completely disinterested. Even if some of the workers weren't too busy, they immediately immersed themselves in activity as he drew nearer. He knew that they had work to do and did not want to be bothered. Officer Worthy had a background in construction work and fully understood the importance of deadlines.

He continued to explore the property alone and his background in remodeling enabled him to recognize something unusual on the lowest level. He noticed that he had to take a small step up to enter one particular portion of the unfinished basement. In every other basement he has ever walked in, typically the entire floor of cement matched in height roughly four inches. The portion with the tiny step was about two inches higher than the rest. Although most of the concrete looked fresh, the elevated area appeared to have the clearest complexion. There were no plans or blueprints lying around to check if it had been purposely designed for some special type of room so he asked one of the construction crew. After asking a few workers and getting zero information, Officer Worthy decided to use some of his authority. He displayed his badge to one of the workers and asked, "Where is the foreman? I need to speak to him ASAP." The member of the construction company seemed to react to the shiny emblem and personally walked Mr. Worthy toward his foreman who had been working on the exterior of the chateau.

The site boss asked, "What can I do for you? You're a cop, right?" The young officer replied, "Yes sir, my name is Officer William Worthy and I'd like to know why one particular section of concrete in the basement level is much higher than the rest."

The foreman was quick to respond. He said, "Some other crew came in here and finished that part of the basement, and they messed it all up. The concrete my guys poured is smooth and exactly four inches level. These guys just went ahead and made the floor in that room six inches. And, if you look at the drywall down in that section, there are uneven cuts and those bums just left it like that."

Worthy inquired, "Who was this other crew?"

The foreman replied, "I don't know. It was weird cause' we've been working this job for close to two months and just the other day we were told to take the entire day off. My boss didn't even give a reason, but of course we all need a day off once in a while so I didn't exactly ask *why* ya' know."

"Do you remember what day your crew was told to stay home?" asked the officer.

The foreman shrugged his shoulders a little and said, "Well it was like five or six days ago. Um, it was Monday I guess."

Officer Worthy's eyes sparkled brilliantly similar to that of child's opening a present. A chill ran up his spine. He said, "Oh' my God. I'll be back in a few hours."

Officer Worthy explained his slightly irrational intuition to the chief of police at his department. The chief and the captain have a great deal of faith in the capable Worthy, however they had their doubts. They said that you just can't go around digging up other people's basements on just a hunch. They reinforced their side of the argument by repeating the name of the chateau's owner, and the fact that he had no specific evidence. The young, competent police officer interjected, "If I'm wrong then I'll pay for all of the damages myself, out of my own pocket. But just think what it will do for this station if I'm right about this one. C'mon captain. I have a strong belief on this one." His superiors reluctantly agreed to the dig.

Three squad cars were dispatched to commandeer the area, making sure that absolutely no footage of the dig would be recorded and then later released to the press. Soon after, the flatbed truck arrived at the site with a huge bulldozer secured to the back. Worthy asked if any of the construction workers present had any experience running a backhoe, and the foreman seemed overzealous to jump on the machine. He didn't want that room to look as shoddy as it did. He had a reputation to protect, and in the competitive world of the construction business, respectability means everything. The foreman fired the engine and rode the backhoe down the ramps. He drove it into position and checked with Officer Worthy one last time just to make sure that he indeed wanted him to go through with it. Worthy nodded to give him the green light. The giant metal teeth sank into the dried cement as the first thrust seized a huge chunk of the floor. Almost the entire police department was on hand to witness the dig. The two agents who were foolishly dressed as construction workers stepped under the yellow police caution tape after they had informed the bigwigs of what was taking place. Everyone stared at the first scoop of debris but it revealed nothing. The foreman maneuvered the machine and tore into the concrete with a second massive scoop. Once again all of the spectators had their eyes glued on the heavy duty machinery as the remnants dumped from its bucket on to the ground. The second scoop was more of the same, dirt, stone and busted concrete. The scene grew tense as the heavy duty backhoe was about halfway finished crashing through the cement and still nothing had been found. Law enforcement didn't seem to notice the bubbly blonde from *The Entertainment Insider* and her camera man make their way down from beyond the caution tape. They were quietly recording live from behind a large tree, but officials were far too engrossed by the moment to pay any mind. The anxious young cop attracted several disappointed expressions, and scowls mostly from his ever-so-skeptic superiors. The third massive scoop revealed the inconceivable. An officer observing from behind the men in charge called out, "What's that, I see something?" All of the onlookers began to point toward the heavy steel bucket in astonishment as it dumped the third scoop of rubble on top of the rising pile. The last piece of debris to fall from the bucket was a contorted human body. It took so long for it to complete its fall from the tall backhoe that everyone who had gathered for the dig witnessed its climactic descent. The civilians and all other bystanders were ordered to disperse at once. *The Entertainment Insider* girl, and her camera man, bolted to their van before being noticed. The phony blonde got exactly what she wanted, footage of the dig, and recognition for releasing it.

The members of law enforcement who were in attendance have seen more traumatic events than anyone could possibly imagine, yet the sickening sight of their city's dead quarterback haunted them for the rest of their lives. His body was naked, and covered in chunks of dirt and stone, but it was undoubtedly clear that it was Hugo Brody. Many of the officers stood numbly in disbelief, but the chief and Officer Worthy stepped near the corpse. The loud roar of the engine propelling the heavy equipment was cut off and an eerie silence filled the foul air. They vigilantly studied the tortured soul and noticed that the corpse still had the chains, as well as the spikes used to nail down its once vibrant appendages, still attached and clanking off of the steel bucket. The flesh around Hugo's ankles and wrists was torn and had coagulated gray blood wrapped around each limb's end. Symbolically, one of the most worshipped right arms in world was detached from his once sculpted body and dangled beneath the bucket by iron links. The metal versus metal friction was deafening to the lobes of the hushed observers as the dead arm pendulum swung right to left. Worthy and his chief jotted down that each orifice had solidified concrete encrusted in it, as well as a few additional notes, and then quickly turned to walk away from the hideous exhibition.

It was a devastatingly depressing tragedy for those who had witnessed the event, but that very moment left a reverberating aftermath of remorse throughout the city of San Diego, the state of California, and for all of the Hugo Brody fans across the nation.

The unedited footage so deviously captured from the dig was selfishly broadcast nationally on *The Entertainment Insider.* It was aired only once for it was deemed too graphic to ever be shown again; however, the image would be eternally ingrained in the memories of those who viewed it. Members of the FCC had to call in reinforcements to coerce the tearful blonde anchorwoman to surrender her treasure. She was only verbally reprimanded by her employer for using poor judgment.

A crumpled piece of light colored debris was lifted from the pile of rubbish by a sudden cool breeze shortly after the discovery had been made. The damaged note was picked up by one of the melancholy members of the police department who could no longer lift his head. He sounded surprised, "Hey, this is some kind of letter. It might be evidence." He went on, "I think it was supposed to be some kind of warning to Hugo or something." The note looked as if it had been buried for one hundred years and sustained severe water damage but strangely the letters vertically that spelled out H-U-G-O B-R-O-D-Y remained firmly adhered.

The captain had a plastic bag to collect any evidence from the dig, so he gingerly slid the letter in and curiously remarked, "He should've obeyed it both times."

CHAPTER 26

Authorities were concerned about who the other construction crew was, but more importantly continued to painstakingly search for Monica Hildeman. Even at Hugo's wake, members of law enforcement guarded with a watchful eye to make sure that she didn't emerge as an attempt to glamorize her inevitable arrest. Her father was already in police custody and Officer Worthy was completely engulfed in seeking a resolution to the murder. The motive was crystal clear. A head coach in the National Football League with a powerful desire to win a game on the world's greatest stage recruited his attractive daughter to disrupt Hugo Brody's life. But, sometime during the undermining, Monica was abused or possibly raped, in turn, creating a deceitful vendetta. He was frustrated that they weren't able to locate their primary suspect. He stood near the entrance of the funeral parlor as he observed thousands of visitors all dawning the same sad expression as they passed by. At one point, the bewildered young officer became captivated by the low drone coming out of the speakers positioned directly above his head. He was fascinated by the sounds of a pipe organ playing the intro to the oldie "Your Time is Gonna Come" By Led Zeppelin. When the song lyrics started, he couldn't help but to think to himself that the song was far too relevant for it to be coincidental.

The fabulous Hugo Brody was laid to rest during a freezing cold downpour just three days after his body was unearthed by police. Despite the miserable weather, the onetime superstar had quite a turnout.

The MOF, Monica Hildeman, eventually slipped up by calling SWAT's tapped cell phone to arrange a secret nighttime meeting with him at a shady service station just a few exits away from The Donjon. Both of their automobiles were blocked by several unmarked police vehicles just moments after they had arrived. SWAT, and Monica were apprehended at the scene with a very timely interruption as the two were sharing an intimate kiss. In Monica's possession was a black briefcase containing three million dollars, which was determined later in court to be only half of what SWAT was to receive for his participation and assistance throughout the vile ploy.

The initial court hearings were overrun astronomically by members of the press. Deliberations lingered for an extended period of time because the court system had extreme difficulty finding anyone to act as jury. Nearly everyone had heard of Hugo Brody, and they were concerned that it would affect the outcome. The proceedings were televised nationally on close to ten channels, and viewers were enthralled according to ratings. As the bizarre and histrionic court proceedings carried on, specific information about the case was revealed. Mike Hildeman was indicted under charges of conspiracy. The withered coach wept on the stand, and begged the jury for their understanding that he "never meant for it to go this far." He swore that he only mildly suggested for his beautiful daughter to "get in to Hugo's head", and that that was all he had intended. He stood up for her cause until the very end, where he finally admitted to paying off over a dozen random people to phone-in bogus tips or leads to the crime hotline.

SWAT was charged for being an accomplice to murder. He pleaded guilty and was sentenced to face ten to twenty years of imprisonment. During his testimony, he conceded to helping Monica escape with Hugo that night at the hospital. He confessed to obtaining a concrete truck, and then aiding Monica in Hugo's atrocious burial as the cursed quarterback struggled for his life. He also faced additional charges, along with his friends Big Cane and Marinky, for conceding to habitually spiking Hugo Brody's drinks with a rare, illegal drug. No one would have ever found out that the used quarterback was under his bodyguard's complete control throughout their entire tumultuous time together if it wasn't for a doctor from the San Diego Medical Center. He testified that while Hugo was staying at the hospital, the doctors on site drew blood for testing. Not only did they find large amounts of the sedative that caused his collapse on the field, but slight traces of a drug known as bufotenin was also detected. The doctor explained to the jury that bufotenin is toxic venom that is extracted from cane toads, and when taken, will produce vivid hallucinations. He also added that it is a devastatingly addictive drug that when it had been taken in combination with alcohol, it would have more than likely enhanced the effects.

Monica Hildeman, who by now looked very much pregnant, was arraigned for such serious felonies as abuse, first degree murder, kidnapping, and fraud. The expectant mother was found guilty on all counts. She burst into tears from the moment she took the stand, and continued to sob for the entire duration that she had appeared in court. She did use the evidence from when Hugo had raped her while she was unconscious, and it probably saved her from facing the death penalty. Her proof was in the photographs, but her case was strengthened by traces of her own blood detected on the mysterious letter that had been seized from the dig. She repeatedly emphasized what an awful man Hugo was to the jury and cried out to them that once her sacred virginity had been raped and taken from her, all she could think about was killing him. The judge, as well as the jury did not react leniently as her punishment was to serve the remainder of her life in prison. At one point, the female judge claimed that it was "dangerous and simply revolting that Monica Hildeman was going to bring another human into this world."

Even though the great Hugo Brody was unknowingly being forced drugs to the point of addiction, SWAT, Big Cane, Marinky, Mike Hildeman, Monica Hildeman, and even the toxins themselves weren't the only components that deserved blame for such an unthinkable cataclysmic downfall. Of course some of the fault has to be placed on society, for continuing to idolize his arrogance. But, if the haughty quarterback would have listened to his coaches and friends' advice, if he would've heeded his loving father's countless warnings, or even if he would have just taken the time to research the ominous letter that predicted his foredoomed fate, then no one would've had to endure another elite, twenty-seven year old superstar's death caused by dreaded overindulgence. When someone has it all, why does a tyrannous, persistent desire to obtain even more continue to exist?

Printed in the United States
147815LV00005B/142/P

9 781440 142727